REBEKAH

Rebekah

A *Novel*

Margaret Phillips

HarperSanFrancisco
A Division of HarperCollins*Publishers*

First Edition

Library of Congress Cataloging-in-Publication Data

Phillips, Margaret.
  Rebekah : a novel / Margaret Phillips.
    p. cm.
  1. Rebekah (Biblical matriarch)—Fiction. 2. Bible.
O.T.—History of Biblical events—Fiction. I. Title.
PS3566.H4856R43 1991
813'.54—dc20   91-70039
                                                     CIP

91 92 93 94 95 ❖ MCN 10 9 8 7 6 5 4 3 2 1

This edition is printed on acid-free paper that meets the American National Standards Institute Z39.48 Standard.

. . . for the charm buyers

Acknowledgments

I would like to express my gratitude to Hassan Abdul-Hadi, head of sociology at the University of North Alabama and a native of the Holy Land, for guiding me in customs, culture, and terrain as I have endeavored to bring the ancient biblical people to life in *Rebekah*; and to my knowledgeable Shoals readers who have critiqued my work with good marks.

My appreciation goes also to my first editor, Lindsey Stricklin, associate professor of English at UNA, for demanding the best from me and encouraging me to stay at my desk.

Part One

Two nations are in thy womb, and two manner of people shall be separated from thy bowels. . . one people shall be stronger than the other people; and the elder shall serve the younger.
—Genesis 25:23

Chapter 1

. . . that's what the Voice told Rebekah, filling her, frightening her. The stirring inside her never seemed to cease, while it swelled her belly to a tiny mountain in front of her. Now, in her tent alone, she held her hand to the twitching, which had worsened during the night, and pressed hard on her stretched skin, wondering that the struggle underneath had not burst it already.

The autumn air was chilly for a night in Tishri, but her body was wet with perspiration. She fought the pain inside her, while the gnawing low in her back, deepening by the moment, warned that her travail was upon her.

But she must make certain before she sent for the midwives. How would she be sure, with many weeks already of her painful, stabbing pregnancy?

She so dreaded the stones, for once upon them she could not get off until her labor ended. And coupled with her dread of birthing her "people" was her haunting worry at their differences, which her body had nurtured, too. How would they be different? What would they be like?

Anxiety dried her mouth, and the night winds of the Negeb, screaming like frightened men north of the camp, made her even more nervous. They always did on nights when they were easily heard.

She would get up and call Mariam or Deborah, quartered to the side of her tent. Perhaps one of them should have stayed with her after all, as Isaac had urged, when he learned she wasn't feeling well the evening before. But she refused his offer to sleep in her tent.

"You need someone with you," he had told her, his warm eyes both worried and grateful. Suppose the birthing is . . ."

"I will know in time, my lord," she assured him, feeling far too jittery even then for her handmaid's endless chatter or Deborah's clucking over her the night through—all her life, it seemed, her nurse had been clucking over her.

She turned on her side, breaking wind to ease the pressure in her heavy stomach, and cradled its cramping with her knees. But a new pain gripped her, held her unrelentingly, and she screamed for Deborah, for Isaac, for anyone who heard. Then the screams in her throat and the shrieking desert winds were one, rushing through her, filling her, as the Voice had done when first she'd heard it, after she'd prayed to Yahweh in her terrible fullness.

It was then the Voice had spoken to her, had told her she would mother nations, that two separate people were in her womb, and that the elder would serve the younger. The words were Yahweh's, staggering in their resonance, and heard by no other, not even by her Isaac.

Oh, Yahweh, be with me in this, she prayed, and suddenly she felt water from inside her trickling under her hips. There was no holding it back.

A mist drifted over her, puddling on her forehead, her arms, her clenched hands. Only her mouth continued to be dry, and her tongue stuck to the roof of it as she tried to call again for Isaac.

Through the mist he walked to her, as he'd done that first time she saw him. She sat upon her camel that day and watched him walking across the field toward her, his striped under-tunic straining to cover his wide chest and shoulders. He smiled as he neared her, a wistful, timorous smile, though in his eyes she saw a subtle eagerness that she loved at first sight.

Upon arrangement with her father and her brother Laban, the servant of Isaac's father had brought her and Deborah to his land. She was made happy to see that Isaac, this stranger, was a tall, handsome man, in spite of her fear that he might not be; and in her eagerness to meet him she tapped her camel on its neck, bidding it kneel for her alighting, then foolishly lowered her veil as she waited.

But Deborah clicked her tongue reprovingly, "Tch, tch, my lady, put your veil back over you. You know not to be forward."

Recovering her manners, she pulled her veil over her nose again, allowing her black eyes, their lashes stiff with yellow desert dust, to show above her black covering. Later, Isaac told her how her eyes danced, how they twinkled when she looked at him.

Now the mist was choking her, soaking her heavy hair, matting it to her forehead. Her body fluids puddled about her hips, and she had no idea how long she'd lain waiting for help when she heard a tangle of voices. Isaac's first, but soon gone, shooed away by women's whispers. Then came Deborah's clucking, "Tch . . . tch, easy . . . easy, right over here, my love, right over here."

Her nurse's hands were patting, lifting, placing her on the cushioned birthing stones. She straddled them awkwardly, positioning her knees as comfortably as she could, while the midwives and Deborah held her upright from behind. She thought of the purple bruises on the women servants' legs after their birthings and tried to turn to Deborah.

"Are you sure the padding is thick enough for—"

"Oh, yes," Deborah chuckled, "we made it extra thick. And from the softest lamb's wool we could find. You're going to be all right, my lady."

Her nurse's body leaning over her shoulders was soft and sticky. There was comfort in her nearness and Rebekah started to whimper, in spite of her resolve not to cry out.

"Don't fret, don't fret," Deborah soothed, limp tendrils of black hair bobbing at her ears as she bent forward. In her tone and touch Rebekah sensed the same concern she remembered from childhood, when she'd hurt herself at play. She turned forward again, settling to her task.

Between contractions, she rested, listening to Naamah's instructions to her daughter Zilla, becoming newly taught in midwifery, and to Zilla's envious mumblings at the brightly flowered rugs and tapestries in the tent.

"They belonged to Sarah, our lord's mother," Deborah whispered. "Our lady sees that we handle them with care."

"Ooh," Zilla cooed, "Mama, look at her vases!" In spite of her pain, the corners of Rebekah's mouth creased slightly. Status did count for something, she mused, half hearing their camp coming to life about her, women and men servants calling to one another, women to their daughters and men to their sons.

She heard the braying and the whinnying of donkeys and knew they were rolling their backs in the dust of the fold, heard the bleating of sheep and goats, smelled their dung and their feet, and with that the morning smoke rising from the cooking ovens. Good sounds, good smells, then not good at all, for a sudden whiff of wheat bread started her body retching.

"Breathe through your mouth," Deborah urged, "through your mouth, deeply now." And by the time the queasiness had left her, Rebekah was numb with pain. Then a jab to her bowels jolted her head erect. She gasped and motioned to her chest, trying to signal that she was being held too tightly. But at her frantic gestures Deborah pulled her even more upright, murmuring at her shoulders, "It won't be long now, not long, my lovely."

Naamah crouched in front of them, and Rebekah closed her eyes to the swift motion of the midwife's thin hands, knowing the first child was about to be seized from her. But she would not scream. She vowed she would not scream, as she'd heard other women do on the stones, nor would she hold back at the pain. She must get the birthing finished, end the struggle inside her.

Heat seemed suddenly to engulf her. Another burning pain split her insides, and she forgot her vows. She groaned in her agony while whispers grew louder in her tent, followed by a sudden silence, then by Zilla's scream.

"Shh!" Naamah scolded. "Be quiet, I tell you." But the girl could not be quieted. "He's got red hair all over him!"

"Our lady will hear you!" Deborah whispered, "barren for twenty years and now this."

"Another baby's—"

"Mama, look! It's grabbed the first one's heel." Rebekah slumped forward, into welcomed blackness, and in the chasm about her Isaac lifted his arms to her, waiting . . . waiting . . . the softness in his eyes drawing her toward him, but she couldn't reach him as she fought the night about her. She could feel her body jerking in sobs, feel the screams leaving her throat, the way they had done on the day she was to have left Haran to become Isaac's wife.

". . . are you afraid to go to this man . . . afraid to go to this man . . . afraid to go with this servant. . . ."

"No! No!" Pain screeched from her insides like the screams from her throat, and the soft hands upon her head were her mother's hands, patting, lifting, pulling the rolled pillow from underneath her head, tilting her feet upward, propping them, clucking over her the way Deborah did. "Tch . . . tch, easy . . . easy."

Then Isaac wasn't there and she was falling upon her father again, and his face before her was first purple and then white and then still and she was screaming out for him.

"Don't be afraid, don't be afraid." That was Deborah. They were riding toward Isaac's land and she was not afraid and no one would believe her and then they were reaching Isaac's land and she could see his smile and his yearning eyes pulling her to him. And she'd left her mother and her brother Laban alone at Haran, and her friend Tu walking alone to the well the way they had done together the day they saw Eliezer there with his camels . . .

So embarrassed he had appeared to be when he had asked her for water from her jar that day. She gave it to him and then offered to water his camels as well.

Tu looked foolishly at her while she ran back and forth with water for the animals, as if some force within her ordered it. And when she dipped into the water it rose to her hands, starting her insides quivering, like the gentle clear waves against her jar.

Eliezer told her he was the servant of their uncle Abraham, and that he had gifts for her family. He passed to her two bracelets then, and earrings of the finest gold.

"For you," he said, smiling a strange smile. "Wear them."

"Oh, why did I not water his camels?" Tu giggled, on their way home with their water, but her eyes had flashed envy. "He's up to something."

"He is just from my father's uncle Abraham with gifts, that's all."

"That's not all. He's got to be after something. Maybe it's you."

"Tu!" She had stopped suddenly, almost tilting her jar from her shoulder.

"I mean for his master's son. You've told me your uncle has a son."

"Two. But one is not with him."

"That's what he wants. I know it! Ohooo, that I *had* dipped his water. But take me with you, for his brother. I would make as good a wife as you, except I'm not as pretty." Tu always teased her about being pretty. Was she?

They raced on to their homes, and she showed her family the jewelry and told them of Eliezer's presence at the well and that he was from their uncle.

When Laban saw the earrings and bracelets and felt their weight he ran at once toward the well to welcome the servant and his men and camels.

"Tell him to bring his men and camels on," her father called after Laban. "We have food enough, and straw for the camels."

He ran his gnarled hand over the jewelry. "The best of its kind," he said. "The very best."

"He's got other gifts, too. For you, Father."

"For me?" He turned to her mother, who drew in a quick breath and looked away from him.

"It may have been a good thing Tu was with you. I don't like your offering to water a man's camels, even if it is—"

"Mother! You know our daughter would always be a lady. This was different—this man was looking for us."

How different her father could never know, for she could not tell him, nor Tu. She could tell no one about the water, how it had risen to her, and the flush of her face and of her body, as if it were ablaze inside while she filled her jar.

When Eliezer reached their camp, he told her father at once of his business: He had come seeking a wife for his master's son Isaac, and he knew that he had found the right one when she offered to water his camels. He said it had been his sign from his master's God.

He unwrapped his other jewels then, of both silver and gold, and a robe for her of shimmering blue fabric with silver embroidery circling it in wavy rows. As she pulled it about her waist and stroked its richness, even the scallops of silvery thread reminded her of the waves that had lapped toward her hands.

And after he and her father had talked, her father handed her a bracelet for her ankle and more pieces of the heaviest gold jewelry.

"Here, my dear. Surely the best of the dowry is for you. I'll keep the weaker for my gift."

She had kissed him then, standing on her tiptoes to reach his brushy cheek, where his dark beard grew high on his cheekbones.

"You're so good to me, my father."

"And you to me. A good daughter, a good daughter. My blessings upon you, my child."

And her mother had run to her then and put a plump arm about her shoulders. "Are you afraid to go to this cousin, to go with this servant?"

"No," she had answered, "I'm not afraid, Mother."

Then they had made preparations for her to leave, and Deborah would go with her, and they had packed their things and had the feast and next morning her father fell there beside the still-strewn low tables. . . .

"Bethuel! My Bethuel!" her mother screamed, running to him, lifting his head, looking at rest of them with fear and pain in her dark eyes.

"We beg you to let her stay another ten days with us," her brother Laban had urged Eliezer after the burial. "Our mother will need her now."

But Eliezer would not abide that, telling them he had stayed far too long in Haran as it was. He began to pass the balance of his rich gifts out to her mother and to Laban as he talked, the gesture signifying it was his departing one.

"You're sure that you're not afraid?" her mother asked again, with loneliness and anxiety and love in her voice.

"Why should she be afraid?" A bit of irritation was in Laban's tone then, the way it was sometimes when he interrupted her and their mother in one of their amiable conversations.

He bounced the lighter pieces of gold and silver jewelry in his hands, but the weight of them was still ample . . . and his own now.

"It is only natural that she take a husband, Mother. And we are sending her to a good one."

"I pray you, then, hinder me not," Eliezer urged. Then her mother's arms were about her, clinging to her, drawing her aside. "It's not always easy to love a man, my Rebekah. . . ." she whispered.

Tears were in her mother's voice and on her cheeks and the wetness lay against that on her own cheeks as their faces touched.

Then her mother's fleshy arms loosened about her and urged her on—to a life of her own, and to a land that had seemed to draw her even then.

But she had never been afraid of Isaac. He had been too kind to her for that, nor had she worried that he was over twenty years older than she. It pleased her, making her feel secure in his land while she struggled to forget her own . . . and her strong father slumping before her . . . and her mother's frightened eyes and soft voice, warning her.

When Isaac was walking so proudly to meet her in his father's caravan she had been certain that her mother had been wrong. It would never be hard to love Isaac.

At first, though, he had seemed so timid with her, or at least to what she would have thought a man to be, from the things she and Tu had heard. But then who were they to know?

Sometimes Isaac must have treated her as gently as the mother he had lost, and whose tent he had taken her to at first, though she had not been happy there herself. The scent of wrapped skin of the aged was about it, in the rugs and in the tapestries, which his parents purchased in Egypt when a terrible drought had driven them from Canaan.

But the scent was ever about the tent, and she hated that. Her mother had taught her clean skin, every day clean skin, and she had kept her mother's teachings. Isaac learned them, too, washing the dust from his body every night before he lay at her side.

She was glad when they left Sarah's tent and moved beside Lahai-roi, where he had fields of grain and servants even then.

And there, that second year for them, the vigor of his nights matched that of his days, as he tended the fields and oversaw his servants in them.

She watched his bending and stooping in his labors, his face seeming to grow browner than it was the year before, while his reddish hair grew even more brittle in the sun.

Dust would cover it and his face, line the edges of his lips in a darker moist streak that made his smile more brilliant. And he smiled at her often as she followed him about the fields, bending and stooping along with the servant women stacking the sheaves.

"My dear, you don't have to come to the fields," he would tell her. "We have servants for this work."

"But this is where you are," she would reply, her answer lighting the yellow sparkles in his soft brown eyes.

Their days were play for her at first, before responsibility overcame her. She soon learned that Isaac's thriving tribe and herds and abundant harvests from the land came with a price, a toll from both their days. But Yahweh blessed them—blessed them together, so it seemed to them both.

And each time they came together in the darkness of his tent she would be certain that this time, *this time*, she would conceive a child for him, for she knew she must. She'd been sent for to conceive.

"Perhaps our first will be a daughter, my lord," she had told him at the beginning of their marriage. She had always wanted a daughter, though she felt certain he wanted sons and impishly told him so in the dimness of their oil light, which, like his seed, was not to be quenched.

Surely, in the wholeness matching them as one, new life of one or the other would begin.

In the yellow glow of the oil lamp, his eyes would cling to hers, as if they would never let go, and in them she sensed his certainty that he would beget, extending himself into posterity. It was what he had asked of Yahweh.

"I'm so proud I've learned of your Yahweh, my darling husband," she told him in the yellow glow. "Glad He has come into my heart."

"Our Yahweh will guide us, my love. Direct our ways, if we keep Him in our hearts."

How she wanted to tell him that Yahweh had been halfway in hers before she left Haran—the water that had risen to her jar had let her know.

But Yahweh had not heard her prayers. Years later, she was still weeping into Isaac's arms at her barrenness and he was still awakening her each morning as he prayed for their children.

But he would tell her not to weep. "God will hear. Don't weep, my love, don't weep . . ."

" . . . don't weep, my love." Isaac's voice mingled now with Deborah's wails. "Twenty years and now this. Twenty years. My poor baby."

Rebekah was swimming in darkness. At times Deborah's tone would die away, and Isaac's would rise, the way it would do in his prayers in front of their tents.

Then his praying had stopped and the cries of infants were about her. Two of them, and they were her own, as Yahweh had promised her. And she was running through Isaac's fields to them, slapping the earth with her bare feet, faster and faster she was running toward Deborah, toward the twins.

And then the fields were gone and darkness was again about her and she was fighting it with her arms, beating her way to her babies.

Chapter 2

 A t last she awoke, coming out of the darkness like an exhausted swimmer reaching shore. Deborah sat beside her in silence, slowly waving a palm leaf back and forth over her, stirring the air heated by coals on her hearth, where the women had warmed water. She looked around from her pallet, trying to raise her head, but it felt too heavy to hold up.

At the gray shadowing on her nurse's face, Rebekah's heart grew cold. "My babies? What's happened to my babies?"

Deborah motioned that she look beside her, where the babies lay covered, and she stretched her arm beneath her blanket, feeling their bodies bound in narrow widths of woolen cloth. But Deborah stopped her hands before she could push back the covers for a look at their faces.

"You have two healthy sons, my lovely. I've already cleansed them, and rubbed them soundly with salt and oil before I bound them."

"Let me see them."

"I tell you there's no way these babies will get infection!"

"Let me see them!" Deborah's face was stern and unreadable for a moment, then she broke into her ready smile and stooped to move the nearer one closer.

She lifted him with a flourish. "He's waited long enough for you to wake up."

Rebekah drew in her breath at the loveliness of him, at his rich black hair and grimacing pink face, at his healthy little cheeks that dented to her fingers. And when she drew him to her bosom his fresh lips found her nipple without effort.

She flinched at his suction, and then smiled as her perfect man child opened his eyes and appeared to look directly into her own. After a few seconds, he closed them again, weary at his struggle for nourishment, and grunted into the warmth of her fleshy breast. And when his lips were still upon her, she motioned for Deborah to remove him and bring her the other one.

"Make haste," she prompted, but Deborah was slow in picking up the second child, clucking to him with a new and different cluck.

"This is the firstborn," Deborah said, with a certain definiteness, easing him to the opposite breast.

Carefully, before the covering was removed from his face, Rebekah turned to him—the one to serve the younger, so the Voice had told her. For a moment she closed her eyes, wondering what it all meant, what would be ahead for her sons. Then another tiny mouth touched her warmly, and she opened her eyes to him.

Tears spilled over her cheeks and along the front of her ears, and she was ashamed to look up. Fine hairs covered his forehead and parts of his face, and hugged his neck like a snugly fitting garment, shaded as the red dirt of earth.

He never opened his eyes to her the way his brother had done, but fought at her breast for his suckle.

At his tenacious grip, followed by a sudden sharp pain to her pap, she forced her forefinger along his thin lips, touching the mesh of fine hair around them. Trembling, she parted them, and then jerked her hand away at once—tiny white teeth lined his front gums, barely peeping through their pinkness.

"We'll use a wet nurse, my lovely. A chief's wife can—"

"No," Rebekah said softly, "no," rolling her head from side to side, while Deborah stroked her hair with jerking hands.

Chapter 3

Drained, emptied of the warring inside her, Rebekah felt a blessed drowsiness over her and refused to move, in spite of Deborah's persistent tugs at her shoulders. "Our lord is here. He wants to see his sons."

She raised her head slowly. Isaac stood at her tent door, for until she was clean from the blood of birthing it would not be proper for him to come inside.

"She's so tired now," Deborah said, waddling toward him, with a baby in each arm. "Two of them yet!"

Isaac nodded, his patient smile widening at the nearness of his sons. And at his back Rebekah heard the songs of celebration, the playing of flute and taboret, and knew he had set the wine to the servants. The women would be whirling their skirts in their dance already, and the men would be jostling one another in glee, and their cups would be lifted to the new generation of their chief.

Now let the virile servants laugh at their lord's impotence, she thought with a smile, propping her head higher on her pallet, watching his face as he lowered it to his sons. She waited for his benevolent expression to change over their firstborn, but his smile did not relent, and as he looked up again he whispered, "Yahweh be praised."

Yet, from the distance, she could feel him reading her own countenance, as he could do so well.

She set her face to straightness. "What names shall we plan for them?"

"Esau, maybe, for the firstborn."

"Esau," she repeated softly, knowing the word meant "hairy."

"And the secondborn, what name for him?"

"That one I'll call Jacob."

Rebekah's eyes widened and her hands flew to her mouth as she remembered Zilla's words. The name meant "grabber." But how had Isaac known about the heel?

"Jacob?" Something strange rose in her throat. Had Yahweh spoken to Isaac, too? No, he would have told her about it—he told her everything.

Yet it did seem as if . . . But the servants had heard. . . .

Her eyelids dropped again, she was too overcome with the day's events to hold them open.

"Go back to sleep, my love."

"Tch, tch, she's done so already," Deborah chuckled sympathetically. "She can't stay awake."

"Let her rest. She needs much of that."

On the seventh day of her resting, as her body healed, she lay on her pallet in wonder, astounded at the strange sweetness she had just learned of Jacob. To think *she* had borne a son without the foreskin and hadn't known it for a week! "Why have you waited so long to tell me?" she asked her nurse accusingly.

"I wanted you to be stronger, my lady." Deborah's shoulders trembled in a slight shiver, which she tried to laugh away. "Well, will you look at me? A shadow must have crossed my grave."

She swept about the tent without speaking further, finding tasks for her hands, while Mariam scooted about, too, in her own quiet manner, laying out oil and clean binding strips and squares of linen. Then she poured warm water into an earthen bowl for Deborah to bathe the twins.

"Tomorrow is the eighth day," Rebekah said, breaking the hush about them at talk of this mark of the saints, from Adam, who was made in the image of God. "Our lord will be getting ready for the circumcisions. You know he keeps the covenant."

Deborah stooped to lift Esau and looked at her with censuring eyes. "My lady, our lord will have the firstborn."

But Rebekah had already slid deeper into her covers, thinking of Jacob's holy mark. And, if a holy mark, then he was a holy child, destined for greatness, a greatness she would have to help him find in her ordinary life as wife and mother.

Tears eased to her pillow, and she wasn't certain who or what they were for. Perhaps they were not for Jacob's holy mark at all, but for Esau's grievous one, although the pain of Esau was not a new pain. It had been with her all week, and would go forever unnulled.

Its weight had sent her often the past week back to her memories of Haran, and she wondered at the sudden rawness in her heart for her family and friends there after so many years in Canaan, wondered if she wept for them, too. Or perhaps her weeping was for life itself, showing her that childhood ruptured into adulthood, and there was no amending the division.

Isaac had not once mentioned Esau's vile covering, neither had she spoken of it to him. It was a thing they would bear together, and yet so separately.

Chapter 4

"Near my shoulders, near my shoulders," she urged Deborah and Mariam, who were pulling a hemp rope over the poles in the top of her tent to swing the twins' baskets.

"You've got them too far from my hands, Deborah."

"My lovely, why should you stretch and strain? We can easily see to these babies."

"I will not have to strain, and it won't hurt me to sit up and push the baskets."

She had insisted on her way, so now Deborah had placed the twins in their baskets above her pallet and already she missed their warmth against her sides. They had become such a part of her now, more so than when her body held them.

She watched the baskets awhile, wiggling slightly at a sudden scream or small bunting inside them, filling her tent with the ambience of new life. And the bunting was indeed slight, swaddled as the babies were.

But at the sound, however slight, she would push the baskets back and forth, until no noise came from within them.

"You are spoiling these babies," Deborah fretted. "Let them stay as still as possible, or you'll rue the day you didn't. With two yet!"

Deborah clucked on, going about her business of looking after the three of them now.

Soon Esau started his crying again, announcing his tenancy in the world as he must have his supremacy within her womb, Rebekah thought. Surely it was this one who did the bumping inside her, as he was doing in his basket.

But his fretting today was at the pain from his circumcision, Rebekah could tell, and she moved his basket gently, humming a tune as she did so, waiting for his screams to subside. When they didn't, she turned to Deborah. "He's burning. I know he's burning and stinging."

Deborah eased him upward with her strong hands, that trembled some, the way they did, as she laid him on the pallet to loosen the soft woolen strips binding his body.

"Be careful, he's sore."

Deborah tightened her lips in slight annoyance. "I know that, my little mother."

Rebekah smiled at the sound of the title and propped herself on an elbow to see how well Esau was healing.

But she looked away at once, for no matter how she tried to smother the choking feeling inside her, the shock of his hairy red body when he was unwrapped was still with her.

He fretted on, screaming louder when Deborah lifted the cloth saturated in henna paste from his sore parts. She laid a freshly soaked one over him again, to hamper infection, then a fresh cloth between his thighs and bound him quickly, from his feet to his neck.

She returned him to his basket and Rebekah sat up to watch, forgetting that Deborah was going to scold her. But she started the basket swaying anyway, back and forth, humming a soft tune, until the noise inside it stopped.

"We'll have to be extra gentle with him," she said to Deborah. "People will—will laugh at his skin, you know." In spite of herself, Rebekah put her hand over her face and wept quietly.

"Tch, tch, don't fret. He will be all right with us. We know he will be all right. Here, let's dry your eyes now, my lovely,"

Deborah comforted, and she wiped Rebekah's cheeks with one of the clean white cloths stacked beside her.

Rebekah looked then at Jacob, sleeping on, undisturbed by any pain from his father's flint knife. The side of his pink face was as placid as a cherubim's, while his raven hair nestled into the curve of his newly woven bed.

She slid back down on her pallet, burying her own face in her skins, tanned on the back to smoothness and tallowed to softness, and she was comforted at the drift of her perfumed oil with which she kept them supple.

Chapter 5

With her purification ended, Rebekah went again among the tribe, leaving the twins in the hands of Deborah and Mariam. She was so tired of her tent after forty days inside it.

How could she ever have stood eighty days' enclosure, had she birthed a daughter?

Twice as long to cleanse oneself from delivering a female. It seemed so unfair, subserviency inherent in their birth.

She smiled anyway at the thought of twin daughters, beautiful little girls with their father's tender smile, one perhaps with her own black eyes and one with Isaac's. One with her dark hair and one with his lighter—

A sudden breath of air stuck in her throat. One with the same skin as Esau? And suppose, if she had others. . . .

She walked faster over the sandy soil, pushing the thought inside her, refusing to let it linger in her mind, and waved at Ruth, wife of their loyal Shuman, who had been with them since his birth.

Pausing for a moment, she spoke to Lothan, sitting under the canopy of his tent already, where he squinted into the glittering brightness of the morning sun. He was the father of Shuman and the first servant Isaac had acquired. She had no idea how old Lothan was, but he was the eldest member of the tribe, and his age held him venerable in all their sights.

The young girls waved to her, ran to her, asked about the twins this day, and then scooted to their own affairs. And Rebekah made her way toward the fields where Isaac and Shuman and the other men servants were at work.

How she had missed her long walks in the open air, and those in the fields, as she had taken on so many days of her pregnancy, both because she liked to walk there and because Deborah insisted she needed the exercise, once she had become so full with the twins that she was cumbersome with her duties. So she left most of those to Deborah and Mariam and Ruth, and walked often.

Today Isaac was in the fields behind the camp, along the slight rises at the foot of taller hills beyond them. In these small fields, he saw that vegetables were grown for the tribe's food. And she had even missed the activities that she loved most—the fall harvest of summer chickpeas and lentils, which would be trampled from their hulls and stored away for the tenting months.

Isaac saw that seeds aplenty were sown for his large tribe, and vegetables aplenty were harvested, because he was a good husband to the land—*and to me,* she thought.

It would be good, too, when she could be alone with him again, in his tent or hers. But then suppose she should—

Isaac saw her approaching and stopped the ox, leaning into the handles of his wooden plow while he waited.

"Such a long walk for you today, my dear," he said, his beard twisting a little to the side as she neared him.

She knew he was going to say that. "I'm fine now. The walk will do me good."

She didn't tell him how much she needed it, for the strain of Esau's unending crying was making her jittery.

How empty and light her body felt! She stepped across the shallow ditch where he was throwing fresh earth into a terrace, to turn the winter rains.

Behind him, servants bent and stooped, dipping up the loosened soil with their spades from the black goat-hair felt. How they could stiffen it enough to lift the loosened soil was puzzling, but they were good at it, and now they poured their dips of earth over that which Isaac had moved with his plow. Working steadily, moving to and fro at his back, they had little time to notice when she touched her lips to Isaac's sweaty, dusty cheek.

Chapter 6

As Rebekah walked back toward her tent, the north wind struck her face with a sudden, moist gust. She knew that soon the rains would start, closing her in the tent with her sons—and her questions—for the better part of winter.

She had been so confused at her promise. The latter part of it was in direct opposition to the rule of primogeniture. It was the firstborn who was supreme in families. But here her hairy little firstborn must not be meant for such right. His brother was surely to have that. But how?

Of course there was the miracle in Jacob, marked already by the saints. But if he were supposed to have the place of primacy, why then did *he* not come first from her womb? It was such a mix-up.

She sighed deeply and looked back over her shoulder at Isaac, for she felt his gaze following her. He was still leaning on his plow handles, watching her walk away.

She eased on down the slope and toward her tent, pausing in the orchard next to the fields. Most of the fruit had been gathered in and dried already, or wrapped in its fresh state for their winter store, except for the green winter figs still hanging on the trees. Deborah used those for her poultices to remove swelling and boils. She mixed the concoction with her healing ointment, too, for all in the camp who would allow it on their skin.

Farther to Rebekah's right a few citrus fruits glistened below the olive grove, where the trees had at last reached maturity. At least she'd not miss the crushing of the olives; that would be next week.

She stepped over a shallow, dry canal between the bare grapevines, where Isaac turned water from the well, digging his trenches all the way from Lahai-roi. And when the sun would dry the thin stream between the rows, servant children poured water into the opened paths, where it seeped into the earth about as fast as it left their jars. But it had counted at the vines' roots, and single bunches of grapes grew so large the smaller children found them hard to handle.

It was from the darkest, sweetest grapes during the vintage season that servants made the wine, and such a happy time the occasion was for them, especially the young people as they pressed out the purple juice with their bare feet. It was a time of singing and dancing and visiting with others their age who came to help from the village nearby.

"Lahai-roi, how I love thee!" she whispered, clasping her hands in front of her as she walked on. How lucky she was—how lucky they all were—that Isaac had so long been able to remain here. And how glad she had been when he wanted to return here from the camp of his father, Abraham. Ab, she called him, for the word was father, too, and she considered him that to her, as well as uncle, brother of her grandfather Nahor.

Ab had taken the young Keturah then, for his camp and for his dotage, so Isaac thought, and so did she. But his mind had remained good even yet, and Keturah must have indeed brought youth again to his body; he had fathered six children by her, and after he thought his time of begetting had passed.

At any rate, he gave Isaac Sarah's jewelry and tapestries and rugs and moved with Keturah to Mamre, while she and Isaac settled by Lahai-roi. She'd had the servants hang the tapestries and rugs over a rope and beat the dust from them in the spring wind, then ordered them scrubbed by hand, so that in her own tent they smelled as fresh as the fields about them, and how very much she treasured them now in this camp where she and Isaac had been so happy.

How greatly Yahweh had blessed them here, though childless for so long.

Here, too, she had received her promise. The sons had come, but the nations waited yet.

Chapter 7

On a pallet under the shade of a large mulberry tree, Rebekah sat to feed the twins. It was a sparkling spring day; purple hills, like jagged pyramids, circled the verdant valley, and she felt she must get the babies and herself into the open air and out of the stale tent that closeted the screams of Esau.

His wailing was with her day and night, sometimes waking Jacob. And sometimes, in her exhaustion from tending them, she would hear Deborah pattering about the hearth of stones, and know she was soaking a cloth in honey and warm water for Esau's ever-moving lips.

"Here," she said now under the mulberry, "hand me Esau. Let me feed him first."

Deborah's face was grim already when Rebekah reached for him, the way it always was at his feedings, for he never seemed satisfied. Whatever he pulled from her was not enough; but she would never yield to a wet nurse for him, for either of them. Her babies were special from Yahweh, and no other mother's milk would enter them.

Esau settled at her breast, and she closed her eyes a moment, dreading the pain of his early teeth. The reddish hair on his body had lightened some, turning to a yellowish brown, lying flatter against his flesh, and the spot on her head above her ear no longer twitched when she held him.

In her arms he felt gentle, tamed, as if he sensed her determination to nurse him, in spite of his teeth marks on her breasts. His brown eyes, with yellow flickers in them like his father's, had finally begun to search her face as she fed him. They did so now, and then he grinned timidly at her.

She loosened his bindings and, as she was finding the courage to do these days, lifted his widening little hand to her mouth, pressing her lips to his palm.

Then all at once his lips parted, the way they would do, and her pap slipped from his mouth. He started his screams, and Deborah looked at her in despair.

"My dear, will you not at least consider a wet nurse from now on? For Esau, anyway?"

"No. I will nurse my sons. I've told you that over and over."

"But I've seen your face when you—I mean, you're under such strain. I'm afraid you're drying up."

"Then there will be goat milk a plenty," Rebekah snapped, slinging the raven plaits at her shoulders and all but toppling her headcover. Deborah could upset her so.

"Anyway, we'll be removing their bindings next week, and they can start eating on their own. That will help."

She laid Esau to her shoulder, but he had not been filled and squirmed against her. "I think it's a shame in the first place," she said, patting his shoulders, "that we must swaddle them until they're six months old."

"You want them to be strong men, don't you?"

"They will be." She meant this refusal to be her last.

But if Deborah wanted to give extra attention to Esau, that was fine; her hugs to his shoulders and tender strokes to his upper forehead had not been overlooked . . . as if the down there could be pushed away, tucked, too, under his bindings.

And it was plain that he would have his father's sentiment. Already Isaac had warned her against showing partiality to Jacob because of the circumstance of his birth. Besides, Isaac cautioned further, Jacob could be as ordinary as Esau.

She knew a mark didn't make a saint, but there was much that Deborah and Isaac didn't know about Jacob. And that Yahweh had chosen to tell only her was still awesome.

Chapter 8

Esau handled his weaning on his own, going to his food with a heartiness such as she had never witnessed in a child, so that his bones became strong and his frame large, surpassing Jacob's in short time.

And when they went outside to their play, she always sent Mariam with them.

"Keep an eye on them at all times," she never failed to caution, and the handmaid would reply, "Oh I will, I will, my lady. If I can!" And she would laugh softly.

Deborah would chuckle, too, at the rowdiness in the twins, but Rebekah saw no humor in their scuffling. Her heart waited in uneasiness, always fearing Esau would hurt Jacob in their leapfrog or their dreaded catch, when they whizzed their small stones at one another, or ram his head too hard onto the ground in their everlasting wrestling.

"Remember to call Deborah to help you, if you need her. And be sure to watch Esau—he bites Jacob's shoulders."

For all her quietness, Mariam was a dependable guardian over the boys. With them in her care, Rebekah went again to women's work. She saw to the grinding as the women servants poured grain into oblong stone trays with hollow centers, cracking the kernels with smaller stones that so perfectly fit their palms. Then they poured the cracked grain, fragrant with its hint of earth, into mortars, and diligently applied the pestles, until fine meal or flour could be measured out for the tribes' daily loaves.

On grinding days, the women set trays of the grain to parch while they worked, nibbling on it for nourishment; and later it, too, would be ground into meal to mix with parched chickpea meal. It made a delicious batter. She liked to spoon drops of it into simmering oil and brown them evenly.

Helping in the grain tents gave her time for thinking, for planning, while chaff from the grain blew slowly aside, like trouble or sorrow pushed away. The weight of uncleaned grain was heavy upon her conscience, too; tares could still be among the kernels. Isaac always warned of tares, which could bring nausea, even death, to the camp.

The servant women knew that, for he so feared the wicked weed he had taught them how to tell it from the barley, and each growing season sent them to pull it from the barley fields before that crop matured. Wheat was a different matter; one could hardly tell it from the tares, so the stalks grew on close together, separated at harvest; but the strange seed made its way into the threshed grain anyway, and picking it out was a tiring task.

"Look at each handful closely. Take the weed seed out, or your children will fall ill," she prodded the women, who would sometimes shrug in weariness at her demands. But it was her job to see they did her bidding, and some of them could not be trusted alone with such a pressing task. Except for Ruth—Ruth could be trusted anywhere. But her place was in the cooking tent. The whole camp recognized the taste of her seasoning and preferred it.

So Rebekah worked often in the grain tent, guarding the health of them all, but more surely one of them. She had to keep Jacob safe, see the end of Yahweh's promise to her, though she tried not to dwell on her part in it. A simple woman like her called to such greatness. . . .

In her simplicity, she hardly seemed the wife of a tribe's chief, for she would never find herself in tunics with braided tops labeling her such. She liked her soft, simple robes. And the jade and sapphire rings that had belonged to Isaac's mother—which he said she wore always—had been put away in her box of treasures.

Her family's food she prepared herself, too, because she wanted to, though sometimes meals were brought to them from Ruth's cooking tent, where all the servants ate together. It helped the peace within the camp, and Isaac watched for that.

Chapter 9

Jacob grew stunningly handsome. She was pleased that his eyes were as black as her own, and others said as vivid.

His hairline was high and well defined, unlike Esau's—with him it was still hard to tell where the hair on his head ended and the short hair along the sides of his face began. But his lower forehead and nose and front parts of his cheeks were as smooth as Jacob's.

And while Esau had his father's eyes, his gaze was not as soft. It early bore a hardness, an intensity that singed one at a glance, while Jacob's revealed a gentleness that reflected his disposition.

She found her pride in Jacob growing as he did, and her wonder at his birth was as intense as the day she bore him; yet, as Isaac predicted, so far there was nothing mystical in his childhood, and certainly he was not without his faults.

How many times she had looked out from her tent to see him huddling with the servants' children and Esau, piling their stones one against the other, until the heaps of blues and greens and golds they had scratched from the earth tumbled before them.

And when Jacob rose from the circle, his dark eyes flashing mischievously, she would know he had made the best trade in the stone swapping, even before she heard the other children squeal, "You tricked us!"

If the bad deal had been Esau's, there followed the threat to Jacob's hide, and the scuffling would begin. But in spite of their sizes, Jacob could handle his brother in wrestling, though when the holds turned to blows, to bloody noses, she intervened—at least when she knew about them.

She knew that greatness awaited Jacob, but she still did try to take his father's advice—to look the other way, to let him grow—though the fear was ever inside her that something might happen to him before she discovered what Yahweh had in store for him.

"Make them something to toss besides stones!" she urged Isaac, but the skin ball he bundled together was about as hard as their rocks.

"It can still put out an eye," she complained, "the way they throw it at one another."

Sometimes she wished they hadn't outgrown the ball Deborah wound for them from wool yarn, before they were weaned; and sometimes she wished those early days were upon them still, as bad as Esau's crying was. At least they were around her feet then.

Nowadays, when they took their leather ball to the meadow, she could hear them grunting and groaning as they leaped to catch it, and when Esau's coarse laughter grew louder and thinner, rising to her tent, she would leave her work and step outside under her canopy, calling them to come closer.

And sometimes, as she watched them walk reluctantly toward her, Esau's shoulders well above Jacob's, she found herself reaching within her, pulling Yahweh's message from deep inside her, wondering how in the world her big Esau would ever serve his brother.

Chapter 10

With her sons growing into robust childhood, she thought her anxiety at their safety would lessen. But by then Esau's daring kept her even more on her toes, for now he *would* have a sling.

Isaac made one for him and one for Jacob, of softened ox hide. But when she caught Esau shooting pomegranates from the top of Jacob's head, she tried to take his from him.

"Esau! Stop that!" she screamed, when she saw Jacob sitting on a rotting stump with the squashy fruit on his head, while Esau stood a ways from him, aiming a loaded stone toward his face. "Stop it!"

But the stone was already splitting the ripe fruit by the time her words left her mouth.

"Bring me that sling!" she demanded, holding out her hand for it. Esau's face paled, his eyes flashed bitter sparks, and he wheeled from her, running toward the grapevines, the sling still in his hand.

"She'll make you give it over," Jacob called after him. "She'll take it if you hurt me."

"My stone didn't hurt you, little brother," Esau yelled back, stooping to pick up another rock. He whirled it round and round in his fist above his head, then hurled it up the hill with all his right arm's might. And then his fuzzy brown shoulders were lost to her, among the amber grape leaves.

That evening, out of the boys' hearing, she related the incident to Isaac, expecting him to reprimand Esau in a somber manner. But he couldn't keep the amusement from his eyes as he told her, "Boys will be boys, Mother."

"You think it's funny, don't you? He could have killed Jacob. Or put out an eye."

"I'll talk to Esau, I'll talk to him," he assured her. "But the boys must learn to hunt and kill, Mother. Remember that."

"Not one another," she muttered, dreading the day of their bows and arrows.

The day came early. Esau began at once to shoot turtledoves and pigeons, soon deeming himself ready to cook them, and insisting that she teach him.

His skill with his arrows and his seasoning—which he learned so well from her that Isaac could hardly tell his stews from hers—pleased his father no end. But it pricked her heart, for when she watched Esau head from camp to the wilderness above them, for which he was too young, thoughts of Ishmael troubled her.

"Does he make you think of Ishmael?" she asked Isaac once. "When he was a boy, I mean?"

"Ishmael?" Isaac seemed surprised that such a thought had occurred to her. "I don't think so. He was raised apart from me, you know."

Isaac seldom spoke of Ishmael, for he had trouble acknowledging him as a brother, born as he was of Sarah's handmaid when the seed Yahweh promised Ab had not come to him in old age.

It was a strange story, and more bewildering than her own. At least her normal childbearing years had not passed when Yahweh sent her sons. Sarah's had. No wonder Yahweh expected her and Ab to laugh, and even told them to name their son Isaac, for "laughter."

Hagar the handmaid was the one to be pitied, sent out with her son to face hardship alone after Isaac's birth. But that was to please Sarah, and Ishmael and his mother were not penniless; Ab had given gifts to the boy, and perhaps to Hagar, too, though Ishmael was bound to become a wild man, living by his sword.

Rebekah sensed that Ab still grieved about that. When she'd first lived at his camp she had heard him call Ishmael's name in prayer at the doorway of his tent, when his laments and petitions to Yahweh would awaken her each morning at dawn.

And she had scooted close to Isaac in his mother's tent, strangely saddened at the agony in Ab's lonely, deep voice.

"Men must always weep for their lost seed," she said to Isaac, and she knew that women would.

"Yes," Isaac said, and his own voice grew deeper, "his has been a strange experience. He's gone on faith in so many things."

"I'm sure our grandfather Terah—my great-grandfather— would have been astounded had he lived to know of them."

"Of course, making and selling his images as he did."

"And worshiping them. He lived for his teraphim."

"My father must have had a special sign though, other than Yahweh's voice he said he heard, to have known he had to leave Haran . . . leave family and customs."

"Oh, I'm sure he did, my lord," she answered, and Isaac looked at her strangely.

It would seem that in the closeness of their nights she could have told him of the rising water, but she could not.

Chapter 11

M*other of nations.* . . . Some days the words were heavy within her. She felt her body wrapping them, binding them, and her heart warned that she keep them there, where they had been since first she'd heard them. Isaac would have laughed at her in the first place, *had* she been able to tell him—if he had never heard Yahweh's voice, he wouldn't believe she had. And certainly, should she tell him now, he would think the twins' wrangling was driving her out of her mind.

While she pondered, at the same time directing the women servants as they poured warm sheep fat into tallow molds, she heard Jacob's screams above the camp.

"He's shot! I know he's shot," she gasped, rushing up the hill with two or three servants running behind her.

How many times she had warned him to stand by Esau's side when they were in the wood with their arrows. Arrows could go wild.

She was out of breath by the time Jacob's screaming led her puffing to him, and then she sighed in relief, feeling foolish at the servants' chuckles behind her. Another mere fight underway. Jacob lay face down while Esau straddled him, twisting his right arm behind his back.

"Give it up," Esau demanded, his coarse voice rising. "Drop it, I said."

"We traded," Jacob gulped, as if Esau's heavy knees gripping his sides left no air in his lungs.

She saw the knife then in Jacob's white-rimmed fist, and recognized it as the one Isaac had made especially for Esau to use skinning birds.

"I want it back! Father fixed it for—"

"Esau! Get up from there," she demanded. At the sound of her voice he looked around at her, surprised at her presence.

"I told you to get up, Esau."

"You'll take it, won't you?"

She held out her hand for the knife, and Jacob passed it to her.

"Here," she said, holding it in her palm toward Esau. "You are both to stop this fighting. Do you hear me?"

Esau grabbed his knife and went running off, while Jacob edged close to her. "Are you mad at us, Ma ma?"

"You frighten me so. You could hurt one another. I remind you both of that so often."

He put his arms about her and kissed her cheek, and then scampered off again to catch up with his brother.

If only Esau had Jacob's gentleness. But he showed little interest in her affection, and at twelve revealed more and more a desire for the hunt.

He grew rapidly as he reached puberty. By the time he turned thirteen he stood a good head taller than Jacob, starting to soar above him like the tall weeds in their fields of grain—and about as much out of control, she was beginning to believe.

How many times since they had entered him and Jacob a day each week to study with a teacher who came to the village house of learning, had Jacob returned to camp well ahead of Esau with the report that his brother had slipped away from the schoolmaster? He was spending time at a nearby merchant's stand that brandished strings of elephant bones and decorated necklaces and small statues of idols. Larger ones stood about, too, Juno and the half-draped Jupiter, arms raised, faces painted red, ready for celebrations. And others.

Once, when Esau had failed to come home, she sent to the fields for Isaac, and they walked to fetch him. They found him standing before the part-man, part-fish Dagon, with elegantly sculptured beard and crown so high and scaly tail curving beneath him. He held one arm upward and one outward toward Esau, who gazed at him with the same glazed look in his eyes that she remembered in Laban's, when he first started his mumbles to the family teraphim.

How proud she had been to send her sons to the village teacher, to learn of simple arithmetic and life experiences, and she had purchased their papyrus sheets and styluses of reeds with frayed ends for marking with the greatest joy, for back in Haran she had studied with a teacher, and in more than one session weekly. Such was a privilege for girls, and she and Tu had walked there together, where trades were taught, too, and where she'd learned more of her skill in needlepoint, which had so enriched her days.

She hoped her sons would have a desire for learning. She wished them to be as sharp as Enoch, with his books of words, though their own lives might be simple ones, probably always that of shepherds, unless . . . unless Yahweh had much more waiting for Jacob.

And here was Esau, turning already from what she so valued for him, and from his father's teachings on their Yahweh.

"What do you mean leaving the place at your teacher's feet?" she demanded, turning his shoulders with her hands and starting him homeward.

"You know better than this," Isaac added, in a tone that, for Isaac, held a bit of ire as well.

And between the two of them, they marched Esau home to camp, with the thought of his new-found interest in both their minds.

"You know this influence is coming right to us from that hill at Beer-sheba," she told Isaac.

"Well, we're not to bow to it." He sighed wearily, and she knew he was becoming worried about Esau now, too.

They'd heard so much about the bestial worship at Beer-sheba. How could she ever keep Esau from one day going there?

Chapter 12

Jacob enjoyed the sessions of his father's teachings far better than the teacher's instruction on ethics and arithmetic. They met perhaps once a week, or perhaps not; whenever Isaac could call the boys together in some semblance of peace. When that happened, Rebekah would take her stitching and sit with them, listening herself to Isaac's tales of Yahweh's people.

At the onset of the months of tenting, Isaac called the boys to work again on their list of ancestors. His request would cause fretting sometimes, especially from Esau, whose interest in the past was easily diverted.

But Isaac had learned to work into these study times gradually, letting the boys' questions lead him. It was a good time for Rebekah, as she listened along with the boys, while he told them the oft-repeated story of Creation, and of Adam and Eve and their Cain's demeaning sin, slaying his brother Abel and tarnishing the earth with his blood; and of a people who had become grossly evil.

"Tell about the lust," Esau urged one evening, and Isaac cleared his throat and nodded. Now that they had passed puberty, they needed to hear of this evil.

"Well, lust was one of their problems. They took wives from anyone they chose, wherever and whenever."

"Lust and brutal violence," Rebekah spoke up, pushing her bronze needle with its crooked head into her fabric, thinking of the ghastly crimes she had heard about at Beer-sheba.

"Yes, the earth was filled with bloodshed, and a people so evil our God decided to wash them from it's face. So He sent the Great Flood."

"This is the part about ol' gritty Noah," Jacob said. "I like this part."

Then Isaac reiterated the story of their ancestor Noah, a great and good man, whom Yahweh told to build an ark to save his family and two of all other living creatures, male and female alike.

Usually, by the time he was this far into a story, Esau would have taken out his knife and begun his whittling, for his interest always lagged behind Jacob's in their ancestors. But so far in this tale Esau had remained quite alert, until Isaac mentioned Seth, Adam and Eve's third son after the death of Abel. Then Esau complained, "Oh, no, Father. Not all the begots tonight!"

"We'll just skip down to Enoch," Isaac laughed. "I want you to remember Enoch. He was a good man, too. Walked with God, and never tasted death. God took him, you know."

"Get on back to Noah, Father," Jacob urged. "He was going into his ark with the animals."

"Yes, and there he stayed, while rain poured down and all of life was swept away, except that on the ark with him. Finally, after the rain stopped, and the dove was sent out—twice, as you know—and it returned the second time with an olive leaf in its mouth, Noah knew the waters were down and he could take his family and belongings from the ark."

Isaac paused for breath, in the long tale. "And Noah did, when Yahweh let him know it was time. Took the animals, male and female, and they commenced to multiply and repopulated the land and seas."

"And Noah's sons started us?"

"Yes, well, one of them, Jacob. Name all the sons, Esau."

Esau couldn't name the sons.

"Shem, Ham, and Japheth," Jacob rattled off.

"And it is from Shem that—"

"Tell about Noah getting drunk, Father. Tell about the wine," Esau giggled, suddenly alert.

Rebekah spoke up. "Esau, allow your father to tell the story as he wants. You can ask questions later."

"We're getting ahead of ourselves here anyway," Isaac reminded them, and his warm eyes lightened as he looked at them sitting on her rugs at his feet. "You know, of course, the first thing Noah did after he got off the ark and was safe again."

"Built his altar," Esau scowled, whittling now on his piece of cedar.

"Yes, and made a sacrifice, just as we do when Yahweh has provided protection for us in bad times. Then Noah started tilling the earth and planting seeds and vineyards."

"Where did he get his roots and seeds?"

"Jacob," Isaac sighed, "he started to grow crops, and that's all we know."

"Some things just can't be explained," Rebekah added, trying to keep the amused note out of her voice. "Anyway, Noah was told to take food of all kinds on the ark, too. Perhaps he did have seeds."

"So," Isaac continued, "when Noah had grown his grapes and made his wine, he drank too much of it." He looked first at Esau and then at Jacob, straight in their faces. "You never want to drink too much wine. Remember that."

"Now you're about to get to the part about us, Father."

Jacob seemed to have forgotten his father's warning already, and Rebekah wondered how the boy could always be so eager to listen to these stories. He seemed never to tire of them, and even as a young child thrilled to Ab's stories in the same manner when they had visited at Mamre.

Sitting under the giant oaks where Ab's tents were, listening to tales of old shepherds, or of young shepherds, or merely the men of Mamre who attended his grandfather's feasts there, Jacob's interest was so whetted that he never wanted to leave for home.

And for Isaac to tell "about us" now, as Jacob urged, was for him to relate the story of Ham's finding his father Noah in his drunken state and, for some reason, naked as well. Ham told his brothers Shem and Japheth, and they covered their father with a cloak. When he awoke he was wroth at Ham for having seen him in such a state, and for telling it. So he put a curse upon Ham's son Canaan. Isaac went through the story rapidly, though he knew the questions were forthcoming, especially from Jacob.

"What about the other two who put the cloak over him? What did Noah do to them?"

"You remember they walked backwards, so as not to see his nakedness."

Esau chuckled and the rusty hair on the sides of his cheeks wiggled as he got up to get a stone to sharpen his flint knife.

"Anyway, Noah put a curse on Canaan, Ham's son."

"Why the curse to the son, instead of Ham?" Esau asked.

"Best way to hurt Ham, I guess." Rebekah glanced at Isaac quickly, and when she dropped her gaze to her work again, she had to blink her eyes to find the spot for her needle.

"Made Canaan's descendants to be slaves to Shem and Japheth's children."

"And that's why we are not supposed to marry Canaanites," Jacob said.

"That's right. We're from Shem. Noah blessed us but cursed the Canaanites, and we're not supposed to mix our blood."

"You believe that stuff?" Esau scoffed, turning to Jacob.

Jacob shrugged. "But what about Japh—"

"Japheth started the Gentiles."

"And Heth was the son of Canaan, so that's why we are not supposed to marry Hittites, either."

"That's the way it is."

"But we can buy burial caves from them," Esau snorted, getting to his feet. Rebekah sensed the old antagonism in Esau that he had always felt for his grandfather, and she'd never known why.

"Yes, you're right, son. Our cave of Machpelah came from Ephron the Hittite."

Rebekah stood up, too, laying her stitching aside. She knew it was time to close the stories out, though if they didn't last too long she found a certain closeness within her family when she sat to listen; and with each accounting, a linkage of her own to a special people.

Chapter 13

Through such encounters the twins learned more of their great past, of Yahweh's chosen people, and a hint of the Promised One to come, greater than them all.

And even though she fretted at Esau's indifference to his lineage, Isaac told her to take heart. "He's just a lad, my dear. He will appreciate his heritage someday."

But she thought ties of family were becoming more insignificant to Esau every day, and he proved it by his carelessness in the tasks Isaac was putting him and Jacob to, now that they were old enough to assume responsibility for herding.

The sheep, however, had not taken to Esau the way they had to Jacob. Their frenzied bleatings always told when Esau was bringing them home, and well ahead of his, "Hoo . . . oh? Hoo . . . oh's?" which rose at the ends as if in question.

"I don't think he'll ever learn the shepherd's gentle, 'Hoo . . . hoo,' " she laughed one hot day as Esau was bringing the sheep to water. His shrieks disturbed Isaac's midday rest under her canopy, rest he sorely needed, with his long days.

"Give the boy time, Mother."

"That's what you always ask for him. Time! Why not obedience? Then try getting it!"

Her heart was bumping in her throat and she couldn't believe she'd snapped at Isaac so. She dropped her head at once, shamed at her sudden disrespect, and he looked at her askance, letting it pass.

By the time Esau turned fourteen, he took to his hunting with a passion, and Isaac allowed it, giving him license to find his way in the open fields, which welcomed him with their coveys of quail flushing at his heavy step; or among the jutting stone cliffs, which made their caves his caves. He would climb the steep slopes like a mountain goat, ready to pounce upon his prey as predator himself.

At sundown he'd swagger down the hill above their tents in a practiced strut, with a still-warm animal draped around his bare shoulders. If weather so permitted, he never wore an upper tunic, and the animal's dripping blood would seep into the copper matting on his arms and chest.

Sometimes Prince would be with him, but mostly not, for the dog had never taken to hunting, though Esau had wagged him home from the hills when he was a puppy. And how the boys had clashed at a name for him, bandying titles that would fit him back and forth between them. Amir was the name Jacob had held out for, because the name meant "prince," and Prince he had become to them.

For the most part, he was Jacob's dog, seeking his company and leaving Esau to his catch, which was brought in triumphant for Isaac's approval. Isaac gave that freely, for whatever befell Esau's arrows.

Then Esau would dress the game himself for the dome-shaped oven outside Rebekah's tent, and it would steam for hours, its savory vapors settling over the camp like aromas from their sacred sacrifices.

Such flaunting bothered Rebekah, and she spoke to Esau about it one day in the onset of the spring following.

"I think you're spending too much time with your stews, son," she told him, expecting his sudden rebuttal, which came without pause.

"What's wrong with them?"

"You know our tribe eats meat only at celebrations, or when a visitor is with us and your father allows us to take an animal from the herds."

"But it's not the same with wild animals."

"I know that, but with your meat flavoring up the air and the servants and their children not having meat, it seems so—"

"Let them go to the fields if they want meat."

"That's just my point. Others don't have your time with their bows."

"You're saying I don't do my share? Who gets the wild honey for our camp? Who?"

"You do, of course, but—"

"I do what my father asks of me." That was her point, too. Isaac didn't ask enough from Esau. Certainly not as much as he asked from Jacob. But later, on Isaac's mat, when she talked to him about Esau's ill manner toward her, she got nowhere.

"He needs your firm hand, my lord," she told him, and her body went a little rigid, as it always did when she tried to talk with Isaac about disciplining Esau. "A son always needs his father's hand."

She had tried to add the last softly, but she felt the muscles in his thick arm stiffen under her neck. "And his mother's heart," he said, starting to withdraw his arm.

Her eyes brimmed with tears. He just didn't know . . . couldn't know. . . .

"How can you accuse me of coldness to Esau, my lord?" She burst into sobs, and her body was suddenly shaking beside his.

He put his other arm about her, drawing her close against him with both hands, as close as he could hold her to him, while she sobbed on, and he said no more.

He was so wrong. She did love Esau. She'd fed him with her mother's milk, with the milk of her veins.

But there was such a difference in the twins, in the obedience of Jacob, as a rule, and the disrespect of Esau. It was enough to break any mother's heart.

Two different people. . . . It was a long time before she slept.

Chapter 14

In Sivan, the sheep were brought in for spring shearing, and there would be another shearing in the fall, a lighter one, before the autumn rains dirtied the summer wool.

Rain had been scarce the winter past, however. Hardly any had fallen. Grazing on the plains had been short, and that in the highlands shorter, which meant the spring wool would be thin.

Rebekah loved the time of shearing, though Isaac clipped his large herds at home instead of in the community shearing house. They would attend the communal feasting and offerings of new wool anyway, where he would sacrifice a tenth of his, but this year's would be lighter than his usual offering.

She was on hand the day he started shearing, and made her way toward the shearing shed. The men had not seen her as she neared the folds, where the dogs lay about, ready to spring for straying sheep that escaped the herdsmen's holds.

Prince, with his big shoulders slightly lifted, ready for pouncing when called, lay nearest her, his yellow eyes alert under his mop of coarse black hair. He looked more wild than tame, and she had feared a wildness in his breeding; but Isaac said he had sheep-herding blood in him, too, because of the ease with which he had learned heeling.

She stood for a moment listening to the bleating animals, ranting in fear under the stirring dust, for too soon the earth had started its summer drying. But when the sheets of wool left their backs, the sheep made hardly any sounds, hunkering as if dumb before their shearers.

Isaac and Shuman were busy clipping, while two herdsmen steered the firstlings into separate pens. The firstlings' backs were to escape the shears this day, and it was Esau's job to see they did.

She looked around for him, but he was nowhere in sight. That boy! How he tried his father's patience, and her own. And now that he'd come into manhood, her anxieties about Esau had doubled. She'd seen his gaze upon Ruth and Shuman's little Uma, and if he should harm her—

The thought was too startling to dwell upon, and so she tried to thrust it from her mind. She must see that Isaac talked to the boy, just as soon as he had opportunity. These strange disappearances, when he wasn't in the fields with his arrows, bothered her.

The work today went on without him, with a servant in his place, while another servant held each shorn sheep by its neck and shoulders, dipping it into a vat of oil that smelled of sulfur and spices and resin, freeing its body of ticks and lice.

Jacob took the frightened wet sheep next, clasping it against his oily chest, gently swabbing its nose and eyes with his soggy cloth dipped in the same mixture, which would help to free its face from gnats and flies.

For a moment he would gaze into each sheep's eyes, seemingly reassuring it with the calm of his own that all was well. Then he would set it to earth again, where it would frisk away, shaking the dip and oil from its back, from the wet, greasy down ready for fresh growth.

His gentleness with the sheep amazed her, as did his forbearance in other matters, as if life itself were a wonder for him, while he waited for each of its unfoldings.

The winters revealed to her even more his serenity, though at his age now the winter past might well have been his last with her, and though much of it was spent outside her tent, for the rains had not come.

But she'd had her time with Jacob anyway; at least, a part of it, as he stood in front of her for hours while strands of flax and wool, which the servants rolled from raw fibers, glided over his shoulders and into thread on the weighted spindles at his feet.

It was a tedious task for the young, one they all hated. But once she got the split yarn easing over Jacob's heavy shoulders he never complained at the standing, remaining so still his sandals at times appeared stuck to her rugs.

"Why do you need the boy to help with spinning?" Isaac complained. She knew he thought the task unmanly. "You have servants enough for that."

"They twitch and turn, and my spindles don't fill evenly," she told him. "Surely you can suffer me to have him from the herds now and then."

She'd had her way with Isaac, and memories of Jacob's tilting the spindles in just the right angle to keep them filling steadily as the two of them worked the day were hers to keep, garnered with her other treasures, while she waited, with him, for directions on their futures.

Not since he had learned the significance of the covenant—that Yahweh expected complete obedience in exchange for His care and protection—had Jacob questioned his holy mark, though Esau despised his own circumcision at Isaac's hand, a symbol that implied, too, the putting away of carnal lust.

But such a time was not upon Jacob yet, and she prayed it would not come. Perhaps his holy clipping meant he would escape that.

Yet, in spite of his holy mark, he had traits that bothered her—one in particular. He was sly as a fox, and Isaac's warning that a mark didn't make a saint found her heart often.

She wondered if Isaac was as aware of Jacob's tricky side as she was. They never talked about it, for though Esau's faults stood between them revealed, Jacob's she would hide, cover with her soul if need be. And she didn't know why. She smothered them to her bosom, to her heart, where she kept the message from Yahweh, and she'd never been able to speak to Isaac about that, either.

Now, she couldn't tell him, for new worries were upon him, upon her, and the twins and the tribe, when they knew.

For months she'd noticed a deepening squint in Isaac's eyes when he looked at her, as if she were not all there before him. And when he had last sharpened her flint knives, he stared at the blades in concentration, then rubbed his thumb over and over their edges, as if displeased with the sharpness. And when he started to hold the knives away from him, at arm's length, frowning as he looked at the sharpened edges, the strangest feeling had come over her.

She knew already, when finally he chose to tell her, that his sight was going from him, leaving him, like the moisture going from the land. It was an omen hanging over them both, but they had not yet told the twins, nor the servants.

"I believe it's because of the tears that fell on my eyes the day my father . . . the day he put me up for sacrifice," he told her one night, while she lay in the curve of his body.

She felt his Adam's apple moving against the back of her head, as if the words still choked him.

"You mean when he—"

"Tried to burn me. You know about that." She pressed even closer into his warmth, into his strength, for hers seemed suddenly gone.

"It was what Yahweh ordered him to do. He thought he was in the right, my lord."

She ached with him, at his present trauma and at his remembered heartbreak. And she thought, too, of Ab's astonishing faith. To lay one's child, one's promised seed from Yahweh, on an altar of sticks. And after all those years of waiting.

She shivered and turned to him. "Your father must have shed many tears over you that day."

"No, they were angels' tears."

"Do you know that?"

"I've heard it."

"But even if they were, how would they be damaging your sight after all these years?"

"I don't know if they have. I just want to know what has, and I thought of them. I remembered how they stung my eyes that day, like boiling water seeping in between my lids and I—"

"They were Ab's. I know they were Ab's tears." Her own eyes smarted as she wrapped her arms around his shoulders. "You mustn't blame Ab, if Yahweh ordered it," she murmured, laying her head upon his wide chest. It was warm and bushy against her cheek, and she lay there for a long moment, while his arms tightened about her.

She knew he was feeling the spurt of emotion that seemed always to pass through him when he held her. But it was not a time for that, and she worked the moisture from her cheeks into the hairs on his chest, rubbing it there with her forefinger, thinking it a better time to question him on the vexing point still troubling her.

"My lord, are you *sure* you've never heard Yahweh's voice? I mean, when Ab laid you upon the sticks, you didn't hear—"

"Didn't hear a thing. Kept my eyes closed so I couldn't see my father's knife over me."

"Ohoo, my dear," she soothed, patting his shoulders. "But you'd think if Yahweh spoke to Ab, stopping his hand, you would have heard—"

"No, I didn't. Just felt the drops of hot water . . . then the burning, and when I opened my eyes a ram was tangled in the bushes, ready to die in my place."

"He bore your burden!" something caused her to gasp. And, trembling, she laid her hand on her breast, over the mad pounding of her heart.

Chapter 15

She was awake before dawn. Her palms were sticky and her neck damp against her pillows. Even so soon before day the heat had begun. It was becoming a bane to their very existence, drying their crops in the earth and burning up the grasses for their herds on the hills and plains.

The servants fanned their faces with one hand while they worked, stopping to pant often, and wondered at summer come to them without a spring.

She raised her head to wipe the sweat from the back of her neck, and heard Isaac at his altar, sanctifying the day for his camp and pleading for a miraculous moisture to dampen the earth, as he'd done for days now. But this morning wind from the steeps of Seir mingled with his groaning, and she lay wide-eyed, listening . . . worrying. . . .

The blue light of early day appeared at last under her tent walls, and Isaac's moans died away, leaving her with her own petitions, her silent pleas for his dimming sight to improve, for Yahweh's protection over them all, especially over her sons.

She prayed every morning for them before she left her mat. It was the time of day when she thought most clearly. But not today.

She clenched her fists, beating them into her skin pillow for a moment. What was she to do? How could she find the right way for her sons?

Any day now, or at the time of his choosing, Isaac could call Esau to him, bestow upon him the sacred family blessing, and he was not the one to lead on in this precious family from Yahweh.

Her uncle Abraham . . . her Isaac . . . she herself, touched by Yahweh's hand, though she knew no more about her promise than she did when she received it. But she could not trust its expansion to Esau. She'd seen the curl of his lips at their sacrifices, as if the charring, perfect lambs were no more sacred than the venison he lugged down from the hills for his father's clay bowl. And he was barely into manhood. What would he be when he grew older?

Isaac kept thinking he would outgrow his sullen temperament, and his careless ways. But she doubted that.

She believed the sacrificial ceremonies Isaac so valued and practiced would be lost to Esau's children. He would not enforce the circumcision, she knew, feeling as he did about his own; his descendants would be disobedient to Yahweh's commands and become lost in a web of the world's sins.

That was surely not the kind of nation God meant for her to mother. But it would be, if Esau's tribe took the family on from Isaac. . . .

Oh, the thought was so frustrating. Jacob's tribe, on the other hand, *would* be obedient. He was obedient himself. One couldn't teach what one didn't know. And certainly he would see they kept the circumcision—he knew the wonder of it. And she its perplexity; at least, his own.

If only he *had* come first from her womb she would have no problem with her promise from Yahweh, her pledge to mother nations, for then Esau would have been the secondborn, bound to honor his older brother . . . her holy child.

And yet, *that* way, Jacob would have served Esau, according to the Voice. But Esau might have already usurped Jacob's place as firstborn within her womb even then. Maybe that's why Yahweh told her the older would serve the younger.

It was all too confusing, and when she thought she had sorted the mix-up out in her mind, she'd run into a wall. Then her mind would rest, and she would leave her problem to Yahweh. He would show her. He would tell her.

She must put aside her anxieties, get up, start her day. She'd gathered in the last of the withering wildflowers last evening, and she would mix anointing oil today. Her oil of spring essence, she called it, which could hardly be that this season, for she was late with it, and the sun had dried so many of the flowers away. But the mixture was Isaac's favorite fragrance on her and she never failed to mix a year's supply for her personal grooming.

And just as she tossed the last handful of crushed wild gladiolus and poppy petals into the steaming oil, she heard servants wailing in back of Isaac's tent. Oh, her lord Isaac! The heat was too much for him!

She ran to the sounds, and sighed in relief when she saw him still standing, while servants huddled about him as he spoke with two visitors. They were Ab's servants, and she knew at once something was wrong.

"It's my father," Isaac said, turning to her. "Keturah has sent for us. She thinks he's . . . leaving us."

They embraced one another gently, while the servants—both Ab's and their own—wailed around them. But she could not weep for Ab. He was an old man, a hundred and seventy-five. He'd had his two lives, first with Sarah and then with Keturah, though his second family had separated him from them in a sense, as second families would do.

But Isaac, the son of the promise, had remained the one to carry on the lineage from Ab, and Ab had seen to that—sending out Ishmael as he did—and even now he'd sent out his other six children, to protect Isaac's favored sonship. But they had received their inheritances in gifts, and Ab had been generous, so she understood.

She wondered if his second family would return for his burial, and supposed they would. Ishmael, she felt sure, would do so.

She knew she was standing too long thinking, for she must start to get their things together. It was difficult to remember what to do in a moment of shock, however, and Isaac turned to her, sensing her sudden loss of control.

"Have the servants put our things together," he said. "See that they help you. We'll leave as soon as possible."

She started preparations for their journey then, getting her mind back to the business at hand. The trip would take better than two days now for their donkeys, and she must carry supplies for making camp.

She motioned to the servants, gave them orders for what she would need on the way, and ordered her oil of essence cooled and stored in her skins for such. The women were not as competent as Ruth, but Ruth was spending every waking moment—when she was not in the cooking tent—looking after Lothan, whose last days also were numbered.

"The twins," Rebekah told the servants, "you must send for them. Jacob will be with the herds, and Esau—have any of you seen Esau?"

They shook their heads. "Try the ridge first, and if he's not there send the children to search in front of the camp. He may be down there, on the plains." How she hoped he was nearby and could be found soon.

But when he arrived home, he refused to go with them to his grandfather's camp.

"He's never liked me. Why should I go to him now?" he asked, his brown eyes defiant as he slid his quiver over his shoulder again.

"Esau, you're coming with us. You are not going hunting while your grandfather lies dying!"

But he did, shaming them with his disrespect, as she and Isaac and Jacob rode in silence with a servant toward Mamre.

Her heart was weighted at the hardness filling Esau, a hardness in his heart like that in his eyes. And he was only fifteen.

For a day and a night, she sat close to Keturah, barely her own age, while Isaac and Jacob sat by Ab. And Ab knew they were there, for between the risings and fallings of his chest, he tried to talk to them.

His frame was still large, though his skin seemed to be shriveled to his bones. And against his raised pillow his white hair and beard framed his face in a shiny halo, as if freshly brushed by Keturah's small hands.

Rebekah was proud he'd had little Keturah for his old age, though indeed she must have had the bad end of the bargain.

While Rebekah talked with Keturah, Jacob had scooted close to his grandfather and had taken his hand. Now he held it gently, while Ab made feeble groans from his throat. Finally, Rebekah realized he was trying to speak directly to Jacob, to get his attention, and Isaac sensed it too.

"He wants to tell you something, son," Isaac told him.

"My . . . my hei . . ." Ab tried to choke out his words, looking Jacob directly in the face, and Jacob turned back to Rebekah. "What's he saying?"

"What is it, Father?" Isaac asked, leaning forward in the scorching tent, made even hotter by the citrus peel Keturah burned to drive away the scent of death. "What do you want to tell us?"

"My . . . my heir," he mumbled. "My . . . my blessings to . . . to him."

Rebekah's heart quickened, as if the message were her own, hers and Jacob's.

"Who's he talking about, Father or me?"

"About you both," she whispered, and felt the movement starting in her chest again, as those of Ab's chest stopped.

She looked at Isaac. Had he understood? Had Ab made him know? But there were no signs on his face to tell her so.

Then, pushing gently the thin shards that Keturah brought to him, Isaac closed his father's eyes, and Jacob stood beside him, waiting to tell him when the shards lay still.

Chapter 16

Fine sand, the color of ripe apricots, sifted under Rebekah's canopy, where she sat oiling her face and throat and arms and listening to Isaac's plan to pull up their camp, to leave the place they had loved for over thirty years.

The sun and wind were blistering, even in the shade. She poured a fresh handful of the oil and spread it thinly over the tops of her shoulders, exposed by her inner tunic, for her body could stand no outer clothing in the heat.

Isaac smiled faintly at the oil's scent, and she knew he recognized her spring essence.

They'd had their time of mourning for Ab, sitting in unbearable heat, and now Isaac was making plans to move their tribe to Egypt. She was not happy with his plans and he knew it.

"Our God will take care of us," he told her. "He has promised."

"Then why not right here?" He ignored her snappy reply and gestured toward the bleached hills, where Jacob and the herdboys had taken the sheep and goats to salvage the last parched grass of the highlands.

"We must do what we can for ourselves." He squinted at the sand whirling before them, and reached out a hand, stopping some of the flying grains with his palm. "Our blessing is that the wind has held off as long as it has, or we would have had no wheat harvest at all."

"But you did get the seed grain?"

Isaac nodded. Seed for another year's crop was collected ritually at each spring harvest, first from the barley and later the wheat. During summer it was dried in the spacious grain tent, then bagged and closed with deference, opened by no member of the camp.

It promised the tribe another year on the land . . . another time of planting and a time of reaping.

"At least we'll have the barley meal. I'm thankful for that," she answered, wishing they could go someplace other than Egypt, and told him so.

"It's best for us," he said. "The Nile waters the land there."

"But so far from all this." She tilted her head to the left and the right of her, in a movement meant to encompass all of home. "Besides, what will we do with Lothan?"

"You know we'll take him with us."

"But he can't walk a step. How can we manage him all the way to Egypt?" He seemed enough for poor Ruth as it was, much less trying to care for him along the way there.

"And lifting him will be so hard on the serv—"

"They can manage that, when they have to lift him. We'll build a litter to fit his length, and two donkeys can haul him between them just fine."

Of course she knew they would take Lothan . . . if they went. And his care would be a lesson for the twins. They had been taught to honor the aged; at least Jacob had learned it. But she still thought Isaac was making his decision to go in too rash a manner. He was not thinking about all that was involved in moving their tribe to Egypt.

She drew in her breath, trying her argument once more. "How can you be certain this is not just another exceedingly dry summer?"

"The signs are all about us, signs my father spoke about, before he took his tribe to Egypt."

"But . . . but I've heard that after a parent's death, one sometimes—I mean, you're not just planning to take us down there because Ab—"

"My dear," Isaac chuckled, "where do you get these ideas? We're facing drought, believe me. We had hardly any early rains and the latter rains have failed as—"

"But the dews—they're all you've ever counted on in summer."

"We've not had enough dew. That's one of the signs. I see your sadness, my dear, but the dryness will get worse. We must do as my father did, if we protect our descendants and receive God's promises to him—"

"But if Yahweh hasn't *told* you to go—"

"He doesn't usually speak to us, you know. We just do what we feel is right for us, what we feel guided to do."

"He spoke to your father."

"My father was a prophet. I'm—"

"You think He only speaks to—to the prophets?"

"That's what I've been taught."

"Must they . . . must they be men?"

"Who else?" He drew his bushy brows together and peered at her. "Why?"

"Nothing." The trembling was in her body again, and to steady her hand she laid it on his warm leg. "Do you think Yahweh always keeps his promises?"

She felt herself shrinking under Isaac's straining gaze. "I mean, I know Ab was *promised* land, but where are his landmarks?"

"From the river of Egypt to the Euphrates."

"But that's unclear and you know it—the only land he ever *really* owned was his field at Mamre with the burial cave on it, and he had to buy that when he buried your mother."

She supposed a burial spot might be all of earth anyone could really be sure about, and commented on such to Isaac.

"And if there is famine, we could miss even that," he reminded her.

She drew her brows together at her perplexing thoughts. "So, you're saying even though Yahweh had promised your father land, all of earth Ab really left to us was a tomb?"

Isaac shook his head, straining to look her directly in her eyes. "Don't doubt, my love. Don't doubt."

Isaac could dimly read her face, but not the inside of her. If Yahweh hadn't kept the promise to Ab, then what about her own promise? Or would that be the way she was to mother nations? Her sons mixing their blood with women of other countries?

It would be just like Esau, anyway, if he continued his distant attitude toward the family and all that was holy.

Already he was sneaking the friendship of she knew not whom, and he was far too familiar with Uma, in spite of Isaac's having bidden them company separately.

"We won't stay in Egypt, will we? We will come home again?"

"When the rains come, and the seasons are better."

"But others could be here then," she said softly, imagining strangers walking where she had walked, with her silent petitions to Yahweh, her silent wails for her sons. "Lahai-roi is not marked off as 'Isaac's,' you know."

And indeed it wasn't, although on the few times they had left it for seasonal grazing for the herds, their spot beside Isaac's orchard and his olive grove had remained unoccupied by others' tents. And when the grass was green again, they had always been able to return there by the well, where clear bubbles gushed beneath green palm fronds, making them feel secure under the threat of summer.

If they left now, they might not be so lucky. She got to her feet and walked toward the narrow open fields at the foot of the hills, the fields that fed their tribe. She looked along her herb bed, lower and to the side, her thyme and mint and sage, the first herb bed she had ever set . . . the first orchard Isaac had ever set, here where they had found a part of earth's permanence, the same as that she had felt in his larger fields at seedtime, when she watched him seeding grain for the tribe.

There was something special about the freshly routed earth, when women winnowed seed behind the men's plows, tossing it to the air to be separated from its chaff. And then the good seed would lay to earth again, to be trodden into it by oxen and men, before the sun soaked up the porous land's small moisture.

She stooped to fill her hands with the loose soil of the vegetable rows and held it to her face. No sweetness of earth was about it, and she sifted the fiery dust through her fingers. It covered the tops of her feet and filled her sandals.

She shook it from her toes and sucked in her breath, almost putting her foot down on a brown lizard that she recognized as poisonous. Its back was covered in white leprous spots and its fan feet clutched the hot soil, its venom seeping into earth from its toes, she knew. It held its mouth wide. She could see the redness toward its throat.

A jackrabbit dashed past, staring at her from the side of its face, panicked at the stalks and leaves dried away. Both it and the lizard would wind up at the well by nightfall she imagined, if such creatures sipped from the troughs there. She had no idea how many wild things did.

But the servants had told her that even Lahai-roi was sinking more each day now, as the sun bore down upon it. Although when she would take her own jar to it, its surface seemed risen, and she would think of that first day water met her hands at the well in Haran, when Ab's Eliezer stood watching her, with the strange gleam in his eyes.

She turned back toward their tents. The fields had brought her no comfort today, left her no peace. And aside from her apprehension at leaving them for Egypt, she worried that, in fear of something happening to him along the way, Isaac would call Esau to his tent before they left and impart to him the firstborn's blessing.

The thought of that day never left her mind.

Chapter 17

In the midst of their packing, Jacob announced he would make pottage for the day. It was to be the final one beside their Lahai-roi.

"And what of the sheep?" Rebekah asked him.

"Father has ordered them to the orchards today." She sighed and turned away. If Isaac had planned to stay one more day, she doubted there'd be a dry straw left within sight of their camp.

"I can watch the stewing lentils while I keep an eye on the sheep."

"Tomorrow, every single stalk of my herbs will be gone."

Jacob's deep eyes lingered on her face, as if he could read her every thought, her every ache, at leaving this place where so much of herself had been planted. "We'll be all right," he said, and started for a cooking pot.

The scent of his steaming lentils was a pleasant change from the heavy odor of wild meat that Esau liked to keep rising from the oven, and she was pleased that he had offered to tend the stew. Now she could take more time with her packing, for the rugs and tapestries must be rolled tightly to prevent creasing, and her flowered vases and special pottery wrapped in layers of soft cloth.

And a final day with him pleased her, for she missed his presence. Lately he was taking more to the fields with his sheep than to her tent. That she was to expect, but at times she found herself worrying over him as he reached for manhood. There were days of late when she'd caught him standing entranced, his mind too absorbed to pick up the questions she asked of him. The situation had become irritating, and she wondered if he would start ignoring her, too, as his brother did, now that he thought himself an adult.

When the pottage was finished, he brought a bowl of it inside, leaning to place it to the center of her straw mat, which doubled for eating and for sleeping. She noted how his arms had filled out, how they'd muscled. His neck and shoulders seemed to broaden every day now, but they were not nearly so thick yet as Esau's.

He wore his gold-colored headband, which she'd made for him from soft wool dipped in onionskin dye. Under it his black hair glistened in smoothness, not at all like his father's and Esau's reddish, wiry hair.

She centered the clay bowl a little more to exactness, recalling the day he had helped her mold it. So quietly he'd turned the potter's wheel on the pivot with his big toe, while she shaped the clay on the slowly moving stone. And the speed of her fingers, when she had pinched a row of trim along the bowl's rim, had intrigued him.

"Smells good," she told him, smiling at the clean rim; he'd wiped away the splashes from his dipping ladle. One would never know his lentil stew from her own now, for like Esau, he followed her seasonings.

Isaac knelt over the mat upon one knee for a moment, lifting his face and his voice upward. "Thank you, Yahweh, for giving us this food from earth," he said, then scrambled to seat himself again beside the mat and turned to Jacob. "Your brother still hunting?"

"Always, Father."

Isaac peered curiously at Jacob. "Well, a boy has to do something he likes, I guess."

He broke off a piece of bread and saturated it in the red pottage, then took it to his mouth with his fingers. He ate heartily, the way he always did, but Rebekah thought lines of stress were deeper on his face than they were the day before.

"I'll keep the pottage warm for Esau," Jacob volunteered at the end of the meal, and rose to leave her tent.

"Make sure to keep it simmering. Esau may be late," she reminded Jacob, and knew there was no need. He knew to keep the heat under it; she was so careful that food did not spoil in this hot weather.

She felt the pride showing on her face as Isaac looked at her. Their firstborn might have proven neglectful, but he could at least be content in the thoughtfulness of their secondborn.

She failed to see Jacob's brows pulling together as he hunched near the warm oven, calmly watching the dead hills above him. And when Esau dragged by her tent late in the day, Jacob was still lying stretched beside the stew, the wooden dipper in his hand, and her insides told her to keep an eye out—he was up to something.

"God! I'm starving," Esau panted, nearing the simmering pottage. Dry wind swept the stew's vapor in his direction, and he sniffed it in exaggerated whiffs.

"Give me some of that stew! There's nothing to eat up there." He motioned with his head toward the ridge above them.

"I'll trade you some of it," Jacob answered subtly. She positioned herself to better see them as Jacob got to his feet, but then continued to squat next to the pottage.

"Trade?" Esau stormed, lunging forward. "Give me that dipper!"

Jacob was too quick for him, jumping out of Esau's reach and out of her sight, although she could still hear them scuffling behind her tent. She could never tell when their fighting was real, going at wrestling the way they did whenever the urge hit them. Isaac said Jacob had the grip of a bear, though one would never think so, his quiet nature being what it was. She pressed her ear closer to her cloth wall, listening to their panting.

"I'll give it to you if you—if you trade."

"Trade what?"

"Your birthright—for my pottage."

"My birthright for—?" She cringed at the oath that slipped so fluently from Esau's lips and pondered what she was hearing. So that was what he'd had on his mind lately . . . a plan to take the birthright from Esau. Possibly he had been worrying for a long time that it was meant for his brother. Or was Yahweh involved in his life already? She knew one day He would be, but surely not in a haggle such as this!

"That's the only way, big brother." Jacob ran back to the oven, and she could again see them.

"Give it here, Jacob. I tell you I'm starving!"

"Not unless you trade," Jacob grinned slyly up at Esau for a moment and then stooped to the simmering pottage, filling a bowl with the red mush. He didn't hand it to Esau, but drew it under his nose, letting the trace of onions blending with that of the other vegetables ease upward, and then he set the bowl deftly behind the oven.

Esau issued another oath, more stinging than the first, and Rebekah lowered her head. "Forgive him, Yahweh," she murmured, as stunned at his language as she was at Jacob's foxy timing, catching his brother at such a vulnerable moment.

"But the birthright is mine. Father's told me."

"You'll trade it. I know you'll trade it."

"What would you do with it anyway? You'll never find favor in our father's sight. Only in Mama's."

Jacob grabbed the bowl again, moving it back and forth under Esau's nostrils, and Esau fell forward, feigning contempt for Jacob's sly bargaining.

"Take it," he panted, holding out his tongue like an exhausted dog ready to lap back its thirst. "What good is a birthright if I starve?"

"Swear it, Esau. Swear it!" Jacob prompted, thinking perhaps as she that Esau's tone was flippant, that his legacy seemed merely an old cloak he was tossing aside, and she was pleased that Isaac had left her tent. At least the bargaining had escaped his ears.

"By our God above, Esau, swear the rights of the firstborn will be mine."

"I swear it," Esau said smoothly, but Rebekah saw the hairy mat on the side of his face wiggle, as if he were grinning inside at his brother's foolish bartering. "I told you, my birthright for your pottage."

"You can't take it back, Esau. You remember."

"I'll remember! Now give me some of that red stuff."

"Here you are, Edom," Jacob replied. And as the late evening sun beamed upon them, Rebekah could imagine the sparkle its rays struck to Jacob's dark eyes as he passed the red mush to Esau. She knew right then Jacob had found another name—which meant red—for his brother.

Oh, that Yahweh would make her privy to such bargaining, she grieved. What did it all mean?

Part Two

And there was a famine in the
land, beside the first famine
that was in the days of Abraham.
And Isaac went unto Abimelech, king
of the Philistines unto Gerar.
—*Genesis 26:1*

Chapter 18

They inched their way toward Egypt, planning to rest several days or even weeks near Gerar, where Abimelech was. Isaac hoped the Philistine king would show compassion toward their camp anyway, as another king had done for Ab's in years past. This present king, so they had heard, was as gracious to wandering shepherds as the first one had been.

Still, in her heart, Rebekah regarded the man with dread, for she had heard, too, that he collected whatever women in his dominion that he wanted. How horrible if he should take her, she thought, with a sudden tightness in her heart.

Her donkey weaved beneath her, pushing her knees into Isaac walking at her side, resting his own tired donkey.

"What if Abimelech takes me?" she blurted, "the way that other king did your mother when she and Ab were in Gerar and he said she was his sister?"

"Pshew," Isaac grunted, "that Philistine king didn't harm my mother."

"But he could have. It's a miracle that he didn't."

"Our history is filled with miracles."

"And in Egypt, Ab told the same thing! That pharaoh there could have used her, too, or those men could have—"

She sucked in her breath at the fright of it, and rolled her eyes in veneration of her dead mother-in-law, twice subjected to such horror, to that special privilege of kings and of ordinary men.

"My mother was not hurt in Gerar, and neither will you be."

Of course he was trying to ease her mind, but the warmth seemed obscured already in the waning brightness of his eyes when he turned his face close to her, so close he could have embraced her on her donkey, and suddenly she wanted to feel the safety of his warm arms.

A burst of dust from the donkeys' hooves puffed between them, and she lifted her veil higher across her nose, recalling that rueful story of his parents in Egypt, both now in the cave of Machpelah.

At least Ab's death had brought Isaac and Ishmael back together on friendly terms, and he had come forward to help Isaac carry Ab to the cave. She thought they had put him away in dignity, too, except for the taint of Esau's refusal to go with the family when he lay dying. It was a final insult from Esau to his grandfather, marking the enmity between them.

But may Ab not know that, she prayed, lifting her face upward and wondering why. It seemed so strange to think the Spirit dwelled in that vast stretch of heat.

But wherever, she prayed It would let her Ab rest in faith . . . in his perfect faith.

And in his requiem he had handed to Isaac—and to her—the charge of carrying on that faith. The thought filled her with uncertainty. Suppose they failed? Or had already failed, in the digression of Esau, in the sleight of Jacob's hand. Mother of nations indeed!

"My dear, you're not listening again," Isaac said. She straightened on her donkey, wondering what she had missed, and clutched her throat. "I'm so tired, so thirsty, my lord. My throat feels like dirty wool."

She could no longer remember how many days they had been on their way. Each one ran into the other, which the servants were ordered to begin early, and well before the pink sky, like a huge dry cup, clamped them beneath it.

Every day got hotter. Until today, Isaac had moved the animals only in the mornings, stopping before hot midday, leaving the afternoons for the herds to rest and find the scant patches of bushes and drying grasses along the cliffs and banks, where the paths cut into the sandy soil. Certainly not enough of either had been found to sustain the animals, and many had fallen to the sands, while the tribe moved on, looking to Isaac for survival, and, in despair, to his Yahweh, brought to life for them, too.

Their progress had been slow, for much time had to be given to Lothan. The morning before they had made camp unexpectedly, having barely gotten started for the day when he had begun to fever, appearing to be out of his head, and was frightened at his surroundings.

Deborah said it was from too much jarring between the donkeys. She applied her cool poultices to his brow and rubbed him with her ointment, never admitting that age was his real problem. And still he clung so tenaciously to them.

Ab was like that, too. The longer his life had lasted the more he wanted it.

But they had only stayed camped a day and a night with Lothan when Deborah and Ruth had deemed him able to move on. Shuman switched the donkeys to please Deborah, tying the litter to the gentler-stepping ones, and he urged the servant boys tending them to keep the donkeys more in step. He himself stayed by Isaac's side at the front of the caravan, watching the way for him.

But this morning the waterskins were empty, and while there had been water the night before for humans and for cooking, the animals remained empty, of both food and water, and now their pitiful bleatings tore her heart.

She looked at the empty oxskins and goatskins flopping beneath the donkeys' bellies, and Isaac saw her bend her head.

"Water is near, my dear," he said. "Believe me." She had smiled wearily at him, hoping he was right. "And we'll stay camped there a few days. You're worn out and so are the others."

He blinked his eyes, as if her face blurred before him. "I wonder if we'll hold out the rest of the day," she murmured, and yet she knew they would. He said water was near, and where there was hope, there was determination.

She glanced over her shoulder at their camp on its feet, barely moving, the women first behind her and Isaac and the first of them her faithful Deborah, now that Lothan had settled down again. Before that, she rode some of the time next to Ruth.

All the women rode sideways on their donkeys, and so did she, for Isaac preferred donkeys for riding to the camels, and Rebekah wondered how the younger servant mothers with children on their laps, or in panniers at their sides, had not become exhausted already. Perhaps they were, she thought. But the children were certainly not tired. They kicked the dust and sang happily when they wanted to, boys and girls together, mixing company while moving in caravan.

Behind the women followed wobbling lines of burdened donkeys, and camels with the precious grain and food and oil bumping their sides. Over their backs Rebekah looked for Esau, but she saw him nowhere. She hoped he was helping with the herds, as Jacob was, but her insides told her differently—for Uma was nowhere in sight, either.

She was about to pass her thoughts on to Isaac, but he seemed suddenly caught up in the actions of Shuman and his son walking beside him, both of them strong, husky stepping, the boy growing to be as muscular as his father, and both their faces set on the distance before them.

She whispered to Isaac, her throat so dry she chopped her words, "Have you seen Esau?"

"He's toward the back somewhere."

"But I never know where he is."

"Don't worry about him. He's not far behind."

"I can't help worrying. You know what—" She hushed at once, realizing Shuman was walking within earshot of her words.

Awareness of the empty, flapping waterskins dried her throat and mouth even more, and she wondered what would happen to them through another night if they failed to reach the well Isaac had heard Ab speak about so often.

She watched Isaac's tired eyes studying the earth, trying to read its directions, and thought how strange a thing it would be if angels' tears *had* caused his diminishing sight. But he didn't know for certain.

Others, she had heard, were saying that it was his punishment for winking at the trangressions of Esau, though she would never tell him that. Shuman was scanning the valley beyond them now as fervently as Isaac, who had begun to sniff the air in quick breaths.

"Master! Look to the side!" the boy shouted, jerking at Isaac's arm. "The trees!"

Isaac dropped the donkeys' rein at once and moved to the side of the trail, which dipped toward a lowland with trees well to the back side of it.

"What kind of trees?"

"Date palms, sir," the boy replied, eyes dancing.

"That's it! That's the oasis." Isaac's beard all but whirled about his shoulders, so quickly he turned and signaled the tribe to turn down, and Rebekah turned back to check on Deborah as shouts of joy went up around them.

But her faithful companion signaled she was fine, clutching her shawl about her trembling head.

Servants and laden animals left the route right away, rolling dust behind them. And when the herds caught up, they took the meadow like a great speckled wave, sheep and goats and oxen mingling, some of them setting to grass at once, while others tossed their heads and stampeded toward the scent of water.

A grin spread over Isaac's face, a grin of half trust, half disbelief that the earth had again supplied their needs; while the servants, one or two at a time, scooted to relieve themselves in a nearby clump of bushes.

Judith, the woman servant whose job it somehow was to oversee the putting down of tents, lost no time in starting her task, laying out her wooden stakes in the area Isaac designated.

"Help Judith get your lady's tent ready," he ordered Deborah, a thing he seldom did, with her trembling a tender matter. "She needs to lie down as soon as possible."

Deborah nodded and Rebekah eyed Isaac fondly, still so very much their chief. Sometimes, when he looked at her from his watery eyes, a glimmer from the past captured her heart, moved it, and released it to sympathy and acceptance of their fate as they grappled with family problems and a livelihood, with only their faith to keep them strong.

He turned his gaze toward the sky, as if he could see clearly the turquoise dome stretching over them, holding yet a part of the sun falling behind distant purple peaks.

"We'll count on a few days here, maybe a week or more, if no one bothers us and grass holds out."

"We'll have grass enough, Master," Shuman answered.

"I'll have to go talk with Abimelech tomorrow, see what he will allow us to do."

The women readied Rebekah's tent, then Mariam set out the essentials for the evening, scooting around as lightly as when she was a young girl. Watching her, while her own back seemed to be breaking, Rebekah wondered by what discretion age selected its company.

She wondered too how many more nights they would have on the way to Egypt, with tethered donkeys whinnying restlessly, forming a makeshift fold around the camp, while they left their protection to their flaming torches and their Yahweh and their men who stood the nights.

Deborah unpacked the straw mat and placed a soft skin over it, pressing the covering smooth. Rebekah fell at once onto it, stretching herself full-length, while Mariam placed a blanket within her easy reach for the night, when the temperature would drop to its usual chill.

Other tents sprung up around her, while voices of women as tired as she filled the air, their nerves pricked by tired children at day's end; and across the valley men and boys were still shouting and running, searching out weak and sick animals, trying to keep them on their wobbly legs or carrying them to water.

The familiar, ordinary sounds relaxed her, soothed her, and she heard Deborah's compassionate clucking again, "Tch, tch, my lady needs this rest."

Rebekah's own snoring awoke her as Isaac was entering her tent. "Esau?"

"No, not Esau, my dear."

"I . . . I must have dropped to sleep already." She raised her head and propped herself on an elbow. "I was trying to find Esau and—"

"You worry too much about that boy, Mother."

"But I didn't see one sign of him when we turned down."

"He's not lost. Just off the trail with his arrows."

"Or with Uma. He's still watching her like—"

"My dear, that's a bit natural. Esau's becoming a real man." He looked away, and in the dimness of her tent she thought she saw a trace of sadness cross his face. "He'll be able to handle a wife all right."

"Hmmph! Wives, more likely."

"You've noticed then?" he grinned knowingly.

"My lord, I am his mother. But let him first become a husband. If he harms Uma—"

"Esau knows better. I'll speak with him again."

"You know what could happen. Shuman could put him to de—"

"But he wouldn't. Uma is not betrothed and Shuman is my servant."

"He's still a father." He rubbed her brow, pushing his thumbs in outward strokes across her forehead, the way she liked to have him do when her head ached, as it did now. She could feel the tenderness in his rough fingertips.

"Rest now," he said, and left her tent.

"It would be just like Esau to take a wife in Egypt and be lost to us forever," she mumbled on in her exhaustion and wished again for home, for their place beside their Lahai-roi.

Still, she had not grieved so much for it as she thought she would. Trappings of anxiety for the present freed her mind from its shackles of the past, leaving her to the hour . . . to the day . . . to the night coming on, and to her constant worry over Esau.

"Shuman could . . . he *might* just put Esau to death," she mumbled on, with not a soul in her tent to hear her.

Chapter 19

She was shaking dust from two small rugs under her canopy when she saw other dust in the direction Isaac and Shuman had gone the day before. She watched until the ball of dust and the donkeys making it drew nearer, and recognized their white legs and feet. Isaac and Shuman were returning.

And when Isaac neared her, his disappointment was evident.

"Abimelech won't let us stay, will he?" she asked.

"He wants us to move closer. Thieves and robbers are too bad out here."

"But, we've not seen another soul here for two days. It's so peaceful—"

"He has a place for us next to the city."

"The scent of our herds near his city?"

Isaac shrugged. "That's where he told us to camp. Grazing is good there, and on beyond, toward the valley."

"But the city will be such a change for us. So abrupt."

"Most changes are, my dear." She was so weary of riding, and had hoped for rest in the quiet valley about them. But in late afternoon, remembering their thirst of three days before, the servants began preparing to move again; and after the waterskins had cooled down, they began to fill them for the next day's journey. But Isaac stopped them, assuring them that water waited along the way to Gerar, where even the herds could drink with ease.

And next morning, as the caravan got under way, rocks jutted upward under the feet of the donkeys, causing them to stumble, and Deborah feared the jolting would aggravate Lothan's condition. But no word came by the servants that he was unable to move on.

Rebekah felt if any of them needed help today, it was she. She had not grieved excessively for home on the way over the desert—she supposed from the strain of crossing it—but today her eyes filled with tears at the slightest thought of Lahai-roi. Unexpectedly, short snatches of her days there would return . . . Jacob standing for her slow-filling spindles; Esau with his daring, his slings and arrows and knives too early; Isaac resting his body and his eyes under her canopy; and Ruth at the tent door when she sensed she was needed.

Perhaps, Rebekah decided, her melancholy was from knowing that now she must make a new home for them all; at least for a short while. And when the city on the hill was at last before them, its buildings strange and uninviting, she felt the same emptiness she had known when they rode away from Lahai-roi.

She had turned her face that morning for a long, last glimpse of the empty spots, circled by tent-post holes, beside the stripped orchard and young citrus trees.

Isaac warned against it, though—recalling, she supposed, Lot's wife anchored to earth in her saline state when she looked back over Yahweh's warnings at her bindings to Sodom.

But, Rebekah mused, her own glance toward home had not been fatal, and she remembered Esau's blunt statement to his father's accounting of Yahweh's turning Edith to salt . . . "just a hunk of salt washed up."

A lump rose in her throat. The scene of the boys in Isaac's tent listening to his story of his cousin Lot was again before her, filling out, growing clear in her mind, as if it had happened the day before.

Isaac had all but made them know Ab's nephew, whom he took for his own after his brother Haran died. And when God called Ab out of the city of Haran, apart from their people, the boy had come with him into Canaan. Yahweh blessed Lot, right along with Ab, and he had a herd and tribe of his own. But then came a division among their tribes and households.

". . . so my father told Lot to choose whatever land about them that he wanted, gave him first choice of pastures."

"Why?" Jacob's voice.

"Because you give the best to those you love."

"And Lot turned away from herding for the evils of the city." Esau's voice.

"Yes, sad to say. There were two cities, twin cities, Sodom and Gomorrah, both wicked, and Lot lived at Sodom. War broke out, and Lot was taken prisoner and carried away, but my father got an army of men together and rescued him."

"Or had the captain do it."

"You will not have it that our grandfather was a warrior, will you?"

"Boys, keep quiet. Allow your father to tell the story as he will." She recalled her own voice, and then her glance at Isaac, as she had tried to hide her amusement.

"But Lot got into the evil ways of the city." Isaac had made a noise in his throat, getting to the part that stopped the easy flow of his words.

"You never want to fall into bad company. Remember that." He cleared his throat, and went on, "Lot fell into the ways of men who . . . who knew men in place of women."

"Must have been some leftovers from Noah's world after all," Esau chuckled.

"Anyway, our God was wroth with these people and these cities, and told my father He would destroy them all. Which He did, as you well know, with hail and brimstone. But my father grieved for Lot, and besought Yahweh to save him."

"And Yahweh told his family to get out of Sodom and not to look back." Jacob always liked to tell that part of the story himself.

"Yes," Isaac said, "Lot and his daughters did so, but Edith didn't. And now she stands where the Lord stopped her for disobedience, in her pillar of salt."

Rebekah stuck her heels into the side of her donkey and looked at the houses of Gerar, roofs thatched with mud and straw and held up by heavy wooden beams. Some of the men were rolling heavy stones over the roofs, to keep them watertight, and paused to watch the caravan skirting the city. Women came to their small yards to watch, to yards about the houses where families came together, ate their meals, listened to stories. . . .

At the edge of the city, Abimelech's palatial dwelling stood on its pillars, and the striking round openings in its upper floor caused Rebekah to shiver, while in front of the caravan a city guard was leading them right beyond it, where its grandeur would cast them as pariahs in its sight.

"Just like beggars," she mumbled to Isaac, as she put away their belongings and laid preparations for the night, while the oven heated for their evening bread.

"A little humility never hurts us, you know."

"Hmmph," she grunted, measuring out her barley meal, ground back beside their Lahai-roi.

She stirred her batter rapidly, recalling that Isaac had told her he could tell when she was worried by the way she beat her bread batter. She shrugged her shoulders and stirred on, whizzing her wooden spoon against the bowl's sides. The round cakes would soon be browned, and she would puncture them and oil them and dip their toasty crusts into Esau's wild honey.

Through the doorway of her tent she saw him tripping homeward, and she smiled.

Chapter 20

Next day, sounds from the shofar came early, as Isaac called his camp to him—in praise of peace and provision, so they all thought. And the servants started toward him—men with solemn faces, women with their heads bowed—to sit waiting, while some mystery seemed to set the air's stillness. *What was to be different in this worship?* Rebekah wondered. What indeed lit her lord's face?

A shining was there that his exhaustion had shut out the day before, a brightness that started the servants' whispers, while they waited in the luminous rays of the early sun.

His expression was as new to her as to the others, for she had not seen his face this day. But she, too, could read his unusual countenance, and its glow deepened his great resemblance to his father.

Were the glistening eyes this morning her Isaac's eyes? Only slightly did they weep today, only faintly did their purulent corners leak.

"First," he announced with vigor, "I must proclaim a message to you. A message from our Great God!"

Her heart quickened. A message from Yahweh. But he said he'd never heard. . . .

"Last night, the Lord God appeared to me directly. 'Do not go down into Egypt,' He said to me. 'Sojourn in this land . . . to thee and thy seed will I give these countries.' "

Shouts of joy broke from the servants' lips, followed by whispers, then more whispers . . . and a mingling of both doubt and thanksgiving, and Rebekah sat in awe. At last, their Yahweh had spoken to her lord. Really spoken to him! And she had not known it. He had not come to her tent to share with her this blessed occurrence that now Yahweh had spoken to him, as He had to Ab, and to her. She drew in a quick breath. Her lord did not know that.

And of course he would not have told her. It was an experience one kept to oneself, for the most part. Unless, as it was with Isaac, the directions were for others, too.

"We will therefore change our plans about Egypt. We will stay here a while, until I talk more with Abimelech."

The tribe was stirring, and Isaac raised his hand to them. "Listen to me. The city will be strange to us, as strange as we are to its people."

Whispers and nods again, especially from the servants with grown children.

"You must be careful. Remember that your children are not to go to the streets without parents, and women must be accompanied by men, even to the marketplace."

Rebekah knew he was searching for her face, and then his gaze settled on her, and a shade of fear was in it. But she thought he had tried to hide it from her own quick eyes.

"Women must dress properly when they go on the streets, and they are to know the whereabouts of their sons and daughters at all times." He lowered his face for a brief moment, fumbling at his great beard, which touched his chest.

Oh, Yahweh, bless him, Rebekah prayed, her face reddening as she looked around for Esau and saw him not. She looked then for Uma, searching among the cluster of young girls huddled together in foretaste of the day. Uma was not among them.

Finally, she saw the two of them, their feet in step, marching lightly to worship. And after Isaac had spoken again to Esau—!

Uma was smiling upward into Esau's eyes and stealthily she brushed her thigh against his when they parted for morning prayers.

A maidservant snickered as Uma seated herself with the women, while Esau dropped nonchalantly with the men. Neither of them heard a word Isaac was saying, Rebekah was sure, and she closed her eyes in humiliation for him.

But when he ended his instructions to his camp and started his meditations inside his tent, Isaac's expression had never seemed more solemn, nor more positive that he was in touch with their God.

He sat inside his tent all day, taking no food, so grateful he was that Yahweh had spoken to him.

Now, he had his instructions. Now, he knew he was of the called.

Chapter 21

Now that Yahweh had spoken to Isaac, Rebekah believed He would speak again to her, give her further directions for her sons. Her heart was heavy with searching as she passed her days, as she walked to the marketplace, taking along both men and women servants, the way Isaac had requested. And sometimes she took Jacob, for he was a good listener to her complaints at the prices of dried legumes and fruits she'd taken so freely from earth, their value escalating now in threat of drought to the southeast of Gerar.

Her days were so ordinary, and she felt foolish at times even thinking about Yahweh's promise to her. Yet, the Voice had spoken to her, as at last It had to Isaac, and he was assured now that he was a prophet.

Why then would she not be a prophetess? Would being a woman void her own calling?

Her bafflement must have shown on her face, for Jacob placed his arm around her shoulders as if to console her. "Don't fret so at the scrawny fruit. If it's what we've got, it's what we've got. We'll make it do."

"But the shekels leave my hands like leaves falling from my fingers, and if the drought stretches on here. . . ."

His trusting eyes danced at her in the sunlight as if all were well. Ah, the young. They were so gullible.

She tucked her arm through his, around the elbow of this son with the holy stamp, marveling, as she so often did, that she had birthed him.

Sometimes she even related him to the Promised One, referred to in the writings of the saintly Enoch, whom Isaac would not have his sons miss in his teachings of their ancestors.

She was certain Ab had fantasized that such a One, perfect in every respect, would also come from his seeds. Yet none knew when or how He would come. And who knew the one to bear Him?

Had it been her? No, no, Yahweh would not give that privilege to a simple woman like her. Her own charge from Him had overwhelmed her. She could not have handled anything greater. Besides, Jacob's mark of the saints had not rendered him faultless, at least not yet—his crafty bargaining with Esau for the birthright clinched that.

But since the day she'd listened to their bargaining, she had seen no outward sign of change in either of them, and even felt sly knowing it. What would Jacob say if she should tell him she had heard?

She looked up into his face, well above her own, saw the calmness under his deeply tanned skin, the twitch, for some reason, of his slightly hooked nose, like his father's broader hooked one. Definitely Ab's stock, she mused.

Her sandals made a slapping sound against the mud bricks of the street as she walked beside Jacob, and she stepped more lightly, trying to soften the sounds.

Suddenly, she stopped, taking a quick glance over her shoulder. "Do you hear someone following us?" she asked him.

He turned to look behind him. "No one's back there," he assured her.

"Are you certain?" Her heart raced in her ears. "I feel eyes measuring me."

She nudged him that they hurry toward home, but he merely shrugged. "Your imagination is running away with you, Ma ma."

"No. Believe me, my son. Someone is watching us."

Chapter 22

"Uneasy again, nu?" Her Isaac could sense her every mood. His strenuous gaze followed her, burned her every step as she circled her carpets putting away supplies from the marketplace.

"And rightly so, my lord. I tell you, those eyes—"

"Pshew," he chuckled lightly, reaching out to touch her thigh as she passed him. But his palm missed her leg by a good hand's width.

Was his sight getting worse? She took his hand, covering it with her warm one and pulled him to his feet. "Let's walk outside," she told him. "Look across the valley."

She wanted to feel him close to her, to share with him the clear shapings of her own vision, the changing emeralds of the hills, their luster declining in the summer sun. And even in that she found reason for worry, fearing it could mean drought was beginning to spread to Gerar.

She wondered how well Isaac could really see the yellow-greenness, or, for that matter, the balls of fleece moving over the meadow, where Jacob sat tending the sheep, and then remembered her lord could see better at a distance than close up.

"I just wonder how many sheep we lost on this move to Gerar," he mumbled.

"Jacob would know." She watched their secondborn sitting with his crook in his hand, like a great young prince guarding his domain, and in her heart she knew with a quiver it was so.

While she stood in the sunlight in front of Isaac, with his full beard brushing her shoulders, she felt his arms tightening about her. He stroked her hair from behind, then rested his chin on top of her head.

"Your hair is still so soft," he said low, almost to himself. "Smells like . . . like the spring." His voice caught a little.

She hurt with him at this unguarded moment. They came to her, too, when she thought about his possible black future.

She pressed into him, close into him, while he ran his hands on down the length of her hair, and she knew she would go right ahead pulling a bit of oil into it, although he had ordered the tribe to reduce their use of it for personal care when they had left Lahai-roi. But after all, she was the chief's wife.

He still called her his pretty Rebekah, and she wanted him to remember her that way, in his darkened day, no matter how many wrinkles she saw later at her neck.

His hands were warm against her hips, sliding slowly, and she turned to him. He drew his hands to her face then, holding it as if it were fragile, and smiled his tender smile, looking at her for a long moment. His gaze held the same hungering that had followed her movements in her tent.

"I . . . I need to look at you more, my love. I need to watch you," he said.

His hand slid again to her hips. "I've not had enough of you, since the boys came. You—"

She twisted away from him, "You don't know what it was like, bearing a—a different child."

"But your childbearing days are over."

"Maybe not. Your mother still had hers at ninety."

"That was one of Yahweh's miracles. You know that. Besides, Esau's hairy covering has blended into his manhood. Now he just seems, well, more of a man."

Her poor lord . . . her poor, poor lord. He pulled her to him again, and his beard brushed her face as he bent toward her, moving his lips along her cheek, tenderly at first, as he always did, then roughly they clamped her mouth, while the passion that must so seldom stir him leaped unbridled.

Feeling his firmness rising against her, she pushed her head into his shoulders, no longer strong, and wept—for the frail shoulders, for the promises pledged and waiting, for the wildness of her firstborn, and for Jacob's shifty bargaining, which she had somehow accepted as her own.

She sobbed against him, wanting to empty herself of the strain of life and of wandering, while he stroked her back with his dear and gentle hands.

And hardly had he left off soothing her when a servant of Abimelech was beside him.

"You, sir. You are the Hebrew." Isaac nodded. "I've come from the King. He wants to see you."

"Abimelech wants to see me?"

"At once, sir." Rebekah watched them go, Isaac's shoulders hovering behind the messenger's as they walked toward the city. She was suddenly filled with the same uneasiness she'd known for days.

She paced back and forth under her canopy, watching the top of Isaac's head getting farther and farther from her, and when she could contain her frustration no longer, took her basket over her arm in pretense of heading for the market, despite Isaac's warnings that she not go there alone. She would turn back when she saw what was happening to him, for she disliked the marketplace too much to go there twice in one day anyway, where the sellers and the bidders tried to outdo one another.

Surely Abimelech did not plan harm to Isaac; but he could do so, if he wanted to. *Hungry men despise another blessed with a ripe wife*—Isaac's words, when he'd insisted she stay away from the streets alone. Would Abimelech think her *ripe*? What a joke. But suppose he did?

Oh, why had Yahweh led them to this place? Faith was such a strange thing, such a troublesome thing even. Sometimes she thought she'd be better off without it, as free and unencumbered as her Esau.

Yet she knew she would not die without hers, now that she had found it . . . , or had it found her? She had never known for sure. But its end she would learn, its finish she would know.

She walked faster, wanting to keep Isaac within her sight. But he must walk slowly, as the chunky servant would discover, and so she would not be far behind them. But she'd keep in the background, to the edge of the path, until they turned into the city streets. And when they did she realized the man was taking her Isaac right to Abimelech's royal house, with its upper floors, where round openings in the front looked directly over the city; or from behind, over their camp.

Abimelech could watch their every move!

Chapter 23

Heading back toward the camp, along the dipping dirt path, Rebekah walked rapidly, glancing over her shoulder as she went, and when she was under her canopy again continued to pace back and forth as she watched for Isaac's return.

When at last she saw him nearing the camp, she ran to meet him. "I've been worried sick, my lord," she said. "What did Abimelech want?"

"I'll tell you later, when we—"

"I want to know now. What did he want?"

"He knows you're my wife."

"Why shouldn't he know that?"

"Because I told the men of the city you . . . you were my sister."

"You did what?" By now they'd reached the front of the camp, and he turned his head to Mariam, churning milk under the shade of a tree. Her stick tripod, which held the weight of the goatskin churn, made a screeching sound as she pushed it back and forth, thoroughly sloshing the milk.

"We'll talk about it inside."

"Mariam can't hear you for the noise of her churn," Rebekah urged, but he kept quiet anyway, until they'd entered her tent, and then she turned on him in anger.

"You lied, just like your father!"

"My father didn't lie. My mother really was his half-sister. And she wasn't harmed in Egypt. The Lord sent a plague to the Pharaoh's court after he'd sent for her, and she was freed. And here in Gerar He—"

"—appeared to the king in a dream, I know, and stopped him. But if Yahweh hadn't done so—Ab lied again—" her eyes snapped in ire "—your mother would have been used at the man's pleasure! Just like I might have been used. How could you?" Her voice trembled in anger.

"But Abimelech didn't take you. And our God stopped that other king in time, so that my mother was not harmed. I tell you He can take care of us, He shows us—"

"I'm not your earth!" she slapped his arm from her shoulders. "You can't read my signs. And besides, you say Yahweh expects us to do a few things for ourselves."

"I did," he said sheepishly. "I'm an old man, my dear, and you're still a beautiful woman. The men could have killed me to make you their own."

"And they could have raped me as your sister! So many times I felt their eyes, or Abimelech's. More likely his in those terrible round windows!"

"My dear, just listen to—"

"I always felt so sorry for your mother, when I heard those stories."

Isaac reached for her, but she jerked away from him.

"Let me tell you what Abimelech said."

"All right. Tell it!"

"He bade his servants see that you are not bothered, now that he knows you're my wife."

"See? They have been watching me. I knew it!"

"Well, he said he'd see no one harms you now. *Or* me. He said they'd be put to death if they tried."

"Truly?"

"Truly."

"And he will let us stay here, right here in the land of the Philistines that my father knew, and use his old wells."

"Abimelech told you that?" Isaac nodded as the anger faded in her voice.

He seated himself next to the wall of her tent, on the fleece stretched over the stack of extra skins where she had formed a couch for sitting, and drew her down beside him, wrapping his arms around her. Did she imagine it, or did she really feel tremors passing through his body?

Chapter 24

In Gerar the summer passed on, fall rains came, and Isaac's servants set out to find fields. Finding them, they sowed in them his crops of grain, emptying the bags of seed grain they had hoarded, no matter how scarce their food had been since the drought that drove them from Lahai-roi had begun.

She had looked forward to the planting, for land was so much more fertile here. Perhaps here there would be food enough and to spare. And by spring she knew there would be, for Isaac was elated at his crops.

He called her one day to walk with him to a field of wheat, and together they strolled toward the miracle he kept talking about. And when they stopped at the field's edge, he said, "Witness for yourself."

He eased his crook into the crumbling soil, and then they stepped into the midst of the tall wheat stalks, with heads bending toward the ground. Isaac broke off a full head and stroked it as if it lived and breathed. Then he reached for her hand, laying the wheat in her palm. "Feel it," he said.

She drew in her breath at its weight. "I would never have believed it!"

Perhaps this was their promised land, she would muse, as the year slipped by, and then another, while their herds swelled with sleek newborn.

Her peaceful weeks were filled with accomplishments. And almost daily now, she oversaw the women servants while they spun new wool or wove new cloth, linen from flax and black felt from goat hair, for the need of new fabric was an ever-pressing one, as grain and dried fruits and vegetables bulged the weakening cloth of their old tents.

Her sons too, would need new tents soon, separate ones, for they were outgrowing the one they shared. And one day, when they took wives, they would need new tents all over again.

She allowed herself a moment's reminiscing, dwelling on the thought of grandchildren that would follow. Sometimes she hardly dared to smile at the thought, while at other times she felt they were already with her, walking beside her, looking up into her face.

If they were too late in coming, she might not be around for them.

But she could not linger on that. One could not dwell on uncertainties; Yahweh had promised to take care of them, and so far that had happened. She gave thanks for it daily, both with Isaac when he prayed aloud, and more surely in the quietness of her heart, where she had a surer grasp of the Spirit.

It seemed another miracle in Gerar to her that the health of their tribe had been so good thus far, that no young among their servants had been stillborn, and only dear old Lothan had they given over to mourning since they'd left Lahai-roi. And he had gone in such peace he seemed not given over at all.

Who next she could not know. Her faithful Deborah? Her lord? No, no, not her Isaac. They had too many things to work out yet, about Esau, about Jacob.

She must talk to Isaac, ask him to consider changing the birthright blessing; she knew she had to do that. And yet she was somehow ashamed to let him know that, by cunning, Jacob was in line for its bestowal.

When she reached that part of her rationalizing, she always

stopped. She could figure no way, make no plan, while she agonized upon her pillows at night.

And the role as chief's wife gave her little time for planning during the day, for prosperity moved her days quickly, which was good. She had so hated the measuring cup.

Chapter 25

They had been in Gerar for a few years now, and the worn area in sight of Abimelech's palace had become home to the tribe. Rebekah had taken the spot for her own, too, with its view of valleys about them, where their sheep and goats and other animals could graze freely.

She was again enjoying her needle, and making plans for it. Pomegranate rinds made her favorite shade of dye, a gentle yellow hue, and before the fruit's season was over she laid plans for the servants to crush some rinds and start a dye mix for her.

Yellow shades were good on her, brought out her creamy coloring. She looked at her reflection in her copper plate, which she kept wrapped to protect its sheen. And in her mind that morning she was seeing a full outer garment with full sleeves as she gathered her bundles of flax yarn she had wound the winter past—though Jacob no longer stood for her spindles.

In her thoughts, the yellow of her garment lay rolled about her neck, and her black hair glistened above it, cascading over the back of it when she combed it out. And in the midst of her fancying she heard Uma at the tent door, with word from Ruth that the dye mix was steaming.

Dyeing flax thread was much more difficult than dyeing wool. The soft wool yarn would absorb the dye so easily, but flax would not. Rebekah could not trust this special task today to the servants alone, and she gathered her spindles into her arms and carried them to the dye vat herself.

"It will make a pretty shade," Ruth said. She and two other women servants worked quietly, as usual, bending and stooping, first sloshing the yarn in the vessel of warm orange-colored water and then stretching it into the vessel of clear, cold water, then pulling it to a third servant, who held the fragile dark thread with the greatest care.

"You think it will be too dark?" Rebekah asked, eyeing the wet thread.

"Oh no, it will be much lighter when it dries, you know," one of the servants said. "A pale yellow when it is woven."

And what a splendid shade for a little granddaughter, Rebekah thought, *for a tiny tunic.* She could feel her needle in it already. Or perhaps she would make a robe of blue, a beautiful blue robe from indigo, with her stitches of excellence on the girdle.

In such planning she heard voices beside Isaac's tent and went to the edge of her own. Philistine visitors stood with him.

After a number of peaceful years among them, Isaac now could sense a tightening of his relationship with the Philistines. They would saunter to his fields to watch his servants at work, observing his fat oxen and his sturdy, outdated wooden plows, with shiny metal tips, far behind their own in design. Still, they inquired into his methods of planting and smiled slyly at the women who followed the plows, their hands flying like shuttles in the air as they left their seed to salute the earth in uniform breaths of green.

"Your herds, too. They grow like your grain," she heard one of them saying now to Isaac.

"Ah," he grinned, in his modest manner, not being one to flaunt his good fortune, "you need only to watch my son Jacob looking after them to know why."

He shifted his shoulders closer to them, to better focus on their faces.

"And Jacob knows the way of the earth. It tells him where to open it for fresh watering holes."

She, too, knew of Jacob's communion with earth, knew his gratitude for its provisions. She had learned that firsthand, on a day of an unusual summer rain in late Sivan, when Jacob was fourteen.

The valley around their Lahai-roi had been covered by a cloud's whiteness all morning, and at midday the cloud had broken into blessed drops of water, then sailed mysteriously away. Grasses about the camp had awakened to a sudden greenness, and fallen ferns among the dust-covered rocks stood strong, waving their fronds in the air.

Jacob was bringing the sheep to the troughs when the cloud erupted, muddying the dusty trail with a sudden downpour, and to the side of the mushy brown path the sheep began to snatch the grass with vigor in the freshened air.

Among them, Jacob turned his face to the sky for a moment, stretching his arms wide, while his long black hair flowed backward at his shoulders. All at once he fell to earth, face down, prostrating himself beneath the sky.

Her heart told her then she could call her second son a man.

Certainly he was more of one now, and had proved himself as a herdsman. He and Shuman and the shepherd boys had complete control of the herds, and she thought Shuman must at times wonder what he was—a herdsman or Isaac's right hand.

And indeed, as Isaac had told the Philistines in their visit with him, Jacob did have the inherent gift of his grandfather for knowing the earth's watering places. How many wells he had pointed out in his young life already.

But once, she remembered, he had missed his guess, if it were such. The servants dug for days, turning up nothing but dry, packed earth, and Jacob was so embarrassed she thought he was going to be ill.

Esau's harsh laughter had hurt Jacob even more. Much to her surprise, Isaac soothed his feelings by lecturing Esau.

"We all miss our opportunities sometimes," Isaac told Jacob. "Don't fret. There will be other chances, other wells."

Chapter 26

It seemed to Rebekah that the more patient Isaac tried to be with the Philistines, the more agitation developed among them for his tribe. Each day a new complaint was heard from the city, bruising the peace he sought with the townspeople, though the animosity had not come to blows. But one day in the middle of his noon rest, Jacob, with Prince yelping at his side, came running from the fields with word that the Philistines were fighting the servants.

"Our men are to let the Philistines be," Isaac replied.

"But Father!"

"Jacob, I will have no fighting among our people."

"The Philistines are closing our wells with rocks and dirt. I can't believe—"

"We will not fight the Philistines. Tell the servants." Sweat glistened on Jacob's face and bare chest, and she could all but see the blood coursing through the deep veins that stood out at his neck.

She knew his muscles ached to get into the fight, too, but he obeyed Isaac's will and returned reluctantly to the wells, this time with Prince trotting close, his feelings as crushed as Jacob's at Isaac's raised voice.

"Oh, my," she murmured, "I do hope Esau is not down there." This day, she sincerely wished him in the hills with his arrows.

Then she bit her lip in concentration, thinking it a good time to speak to Isaac about the birthright blessing, ask him to consider it for Jacob. There was such a difference in the twins. And so much to tell him Jacob was the one for it . . . the way Jacob had responded to his wishes just now, for one thing.

Esau would never have done that—he would never have come to tell them of the fighting in the first place, but joined right in it, enjoying every minute of it.

And there was Ab's message to them in his dying breath.

Perhaps if she just dared open the subject now. But as she mustered nerve enough to begin, a servant appeared, announcing visitors to the camp.

A second time Isaac trudged toward the king's quarters, and something told her already what Abimelech would have to say.

"He wants us to leave," Isaac sighed, when he had returned from the palace. "Says the Philistines are too jealous—"

"Jealous? Of our simple ways? They, in their houses, jealous of shepherds' tents?"

"Jealous of our God, of the favor He shows us."

"Where did you tell him we'd go? Yahweh told you not to go to Egypt."

"Farther down the Gerar valley. My father dug wells there, too, and we'll have enough grass."

"Will we always keep moving when trouble comes?"

"We are a people of good will. We'll start over again."

"How many times can we do that?"

Chapter 27

Within a few days they were again on their donkeys, their belongings bumping the animals' sides as the tribe treaded out the way of peace. Jacob and Shuman and the other servants were with the herds, keeping the large number of animals in this difficult exit from the city's edge, so Isaac had bidden Esau walk at his side in front of the caravan. Esau, too, could read earth's language with great accuracy.

Shortly out of Gerar, they veered southwest, where they camped for the night. The next day they started at a snail's pace toward the valley beyond Gerar, with Isaac straining his eyes for small mounds of grassed-over earth with low spots beside them which would tell of his father's lost wells.

Because Jacob was needed with the herds and was nowhere near the front of the caravan, Esau had not quarreled at his father's request to help search out the green spots. More and more, Rebekah was aware that her sons were indeed separate people. A while ago they needed separate tents; now they needed separate space.

Heading the caravan was a new experience for Esau, and he lifted his eyes to the far hills and plains often. Rebekah knew that as soon as they had found the wells and the caravan was settled again, he would head back to his arrows, feigning excuses to keep from helping the servants with the digging.

When the first well was sighted and tents set up for what Rebekah could tell was meant to be a period of time, she felt uneasy, and inquired of Isaac if they were far enough from the Philistines.

"We'll be safe enough out here," he said. "Just have to wait and see what happens. The grass is too good to pass up."

As the old wells of his father were discovered and reopened, Isaac gave to each the name originally assigned to it, for he had been taught that the name of a well was of great significance. But Rebekah was certain the water itself was of less significance, for it tasted of impurities and Shuman said it was too shallow in the ground.

"We'll need new wells, Master," he told Isaac.

"Then dig," Isaac advised. "Dig a new well." This the servants did, unearthing a stream of endless flow; but the report of it brought the Philistines on them in fury.

The water was their own, they insisted, so Isaac agreed to let them have it, too tired too argue with them and too aggravated to give the well a name. Then, on second thought, he declared its title to be "Esek," since it was a well of argument.

Once more, another campsite, another well, only to have it rendered the same treatment by the Philistines, to which Isaac turned aside again.

"You are turning too much to peace, Master," Shuman ventured to suggest.

"So let us call this well 'Sitnah,' then, well of anger!" Isaac stormed, irked that Shuman would dare call his hand on a decision so important to him.

Finally, another campsite was settled into, and another place for digging decided upon, this time between Isaac and Jacob, and Isaac shuffled his feet along the ground and said, "Dig it about here. I say the earth has room and water enough for all of us."

Nevertheless, when water was freely springing from it, watering with ease their whole camp, Rebekah watched for days, fearing the Philistines at their door again, while Isaac scoured the valley as best he could, holding the sun from his eyes with his hands and making every approaching figure to be that of a quarrelsome Philistine.

When none came, he vowed with relief that this third well would be called "Rehoboth," for their God had made room for them all.

Chapter 28

The Philistines at last chose to let Isaac's abundance of water pass, but the tribe's fighting with them had not completely ceased. Rebekah doubted that it would ever do so now, for once enemies were made, they were not easily disposed of. And even though months had passed when she heard of the continuing disputes among them and the servants and saw Esau's bloody chest as he returned from his wrangles with them, she knew peace was a long way from the camp.

Esau's eyes glistened after such excursions, setting fear in her heart, while Jacob taunted, "Edom, Edom," whenever he had the chance.

She was almost thankful Isaac could not see the fiery glances they flashed one another in their squabbling, and realized, with a tinge of despair, that only distance now could still the "differences" that lay ever between them.

But while time wore on, she decided Isaac might know as much as she did about their quarreling and was as concerned about them as she. At least he was troubled deeply about something. He stayed too long in the sun . . . in the fields, crossing the gullies there on his own, with only the aid of his crook. But he *would* go there.

And when he returned, a deep somberness would be on his face, or some loneliness that broke her heart, and by the time he came to her with his feelings—one day when the servants were harvesting wheat—she had decided he was pondering more than family problems.

Before he spoke, she knew they would be pulling up their tents.

"I want to move our people again, my love."

"Where now? I'm so tired of moving," she answered wearily.

"I want to take them home."

"Home?" She thought she would never hear those words again.

"When the harvest is in, we'll go back to my father's land—"

"To the field with the burial ca—"

"No, no. Not that land."

"You mean back to Lahai-roi!"

"No, not there."

"But you said—"

"I doubt there's room enough for us at Lahai-roi, the Lord has blessed us too soundly. We'll go to Beer-sheba."

"Oh," she whispered, remembering her mother had told her men wanted to go home to die. Isaac was born at Beer-sheba. He had grown up there.

"We'll go to my father's great well. It represents a pact between my father and the Philistines of his day."

"But that's not with us, and—"

"Abimelech will honor the treaty of my father there, and the warring among our people will stop."

He sat thinking for a moment, his stiff knees drawn to a point in front of him, for no longer would they fit before him crossed. "We must guard our crops and our people here. It is not good, and Esau continues to come home from his ready fights."

"My lord, I didn't know you could . . . you had seen the blood."

"I can smell Esau, my dear. I know when he's been fighting."

Of course he knew. She sometimes forgot his sensitive nose, put to double use now with his vanishing sight. She had at last accepted that his sight was going—or at least she had stopped fighting against it inside, as Isaac had finally done, and now they were trying to make the best of things. One did that, she had learned, when there was no other alternative.

Such a look of submissiveness was on Isaac's face as they talked that she thought it the very time to broach the sensitive subject that never left her mind.

She knew Isaac had been disturbed at Ab's last words to them about Jacob . . . about Ab's appointing him heir. But even so, she feared if she asked Isaac to consider switching the blessing, he would only tell her, "First in sons, first in blessings."

And though they might be able to talk about Jacob's place in her womb having been usurped by Esau, as she was certain happened, she still might not be able to tell him of the Voice, of the message. It had been wrapped too long inside her.

"My . . . my lord," she said, fumbling her fingers in her lap as she sat next to him on her low couch of folded skins. "We need to talk."

But he seemed not to have heard her. The seepage from his eyes was heavier today, when he turned his face in the direction of Beer-sheba.

"We'll start as soon as the grain is in," he said. She put her arms about him, drawing his head toward her bosom.

"How very tired you are, my lord," she whispered, and rocked her shoulders gently.

Part Three

And he went up from
thence to Beer-sheba.
—*Genesis 26:23*

Chapter 29

Again, Isaac called forth Esau to walk beside him at the head of the caravan, and Esau came forward to claim the honorable place he had laid to waste for years. Isaac's pleasure at having him there made it plain to Rebekah that their firstborn was still first in his father's heart, hence the treasured family blessing, which he would prostitute to his own ill will.

She was aware of the way the fuzzy hair lay warm against his bare arms and shoulders, like a shield for his hunt, while the copper bristles on his chest stood firmer, his long strides barely winding him.

His bow was at his back. His short deerskin skirt, with which he wrapped his loins regularly now in spring and summer, exchanging it only for his goatskin skirt in winter, fell solidly over his heavy hips.

Calmly, he watched the route before them, his thick shoulders erect as he called out the landmarks at his father's ear, laughing with him at shared trivia of the day.

What a robust, carnal man her Esau had become, she thought. With so many secrets locked inside him.

Certainly, as his father had said, he had long been ready for a wife, and they must start plans for that as soon as they got situated at Beer-sheba. But she doubted Esau would cooperate with their selection in a mate.

As for Jacob, he had revealed no outward signs of being ready for marriage. For months, she had run her hands over his bedding when she cleaned it, expecting to find the same evidence of manhood there that she found on Esau's.

But so far, she had no choice except a mother's—to wonder at Jacob's virility, and she prayed his sacred mark would not restrict him to celibacy.

Oh, Yahweh! Would that she not mother nations through her Esau alone.

Chapter 30

Each settling-in after a journey left her sorer than the one before, Rebekah thought, sighing. She was dressing for the special worship Isaac had called in praise of Yahweh's protection and guidance. Here, at Beer-sheba, they would be offering a sacrifice.

Although her arms and legs were stiff as she made her way to the altar ahead of the servants, she felt comfort in her insides, and that was what mattered when they camped in a new location.

A soft wind touched her face, sifting peace through her, and a soothing scent of the herds was fresh about her as the animals stirred and stretched, leaving steamy droppings in the humors of first day. Some of the donkeys opened their mouths to the morning air, braying in satisfaction at a day's rest, while others rolled in the dust, turning first to one side and then the other in their leisure.

She seated herself before Isaac, who waited for them beyond his charring, perfect lamb, prepared for him by the servants. But she smiled wistfully at the uneven heap of stones, knowing he had laid the altar himself.

And when she saw the hallowed sheen on his face, she knew he'd heard again from Yahweh; the same elation glowed there as before in Gerar when Yahweh spoke to him, perhaps today an even greater radiance.

"My people," he moved his face from one side to the other, trying to grasp the servants' positions in front of him, "I want you to know our God has appeared to me again in the night. My seed are to be numbered here in this land for my father Abraham's sake."

Rebekah waited for the whispers, for the giggles. But she heard no laughter, saw no stirring, only pensive, meditative faces that watched her lord while swirls of dark, sweet-scented meat smoke from the sacrificial lamb fell backward upon them.

"This move was right for us. This is where we will stay," he said. And now their ceremony evolved into celebration, while swelling sounds of their festivity filled the air.

Later, she and Isaac walked the short distance to her tent, and a sweet zephyr from the date palms at the great well's mouth came to them, incensing their nostrils with the earthy scent of water and cool moss. Ab had called it the "Well of Oath," which was also "Beer-sheba," and the very atmosphere around it commemorated peace.

The thought of Ab's camp here before their own warmed her, thrilled her. Family most surely was one's most magnificent asset, she believed, and Yahweh had promised to nurture Ab's, a pledge extended now to her lord in the fosterage of his own seed.

It was enough to cause one to smile, and she pressed Isaac's hand with her fingers and struck her feet harder on the ground where his parents had walked before her. Already, she felt a timelessness in the shadow of their steps, as she eyed the grove of cedars to the left of her that Ab had set.

She insisted Isaac rest for the balance of the day, which had started for him well before dawn, and he stretched himself upon the skins in her tent. Sounds of celebration continued about them, while the servants sang and danced, and rejoiced at peace and plenty.

But next day, when the servants were again in their places and the smoky drift from their sacrifice and their feasting lay in the air still, Shuman came to Isaac's tent.

"We have measured the well, Master," he said. "It will never water our herds. We have the smaller wells farther out, but the great one has filled too much."

"Then dig it deeper," Isaac ordered. "I know the water is there. It is the well of my father."

His face was rapturous with his faith. "Dig until you have water enough, no matter how long it takes."

And as his servants dug, Isaac sat reconciled to his surroundings, at ease in his newly found peace, although Rebekah was disturbed at it. Why did she fear his time to go was nearing? She mustn't. His health was good, except for his ruptured sight. She should rejoice in his good health; and he had servants to help with his sight.

A few days later, still pondering these questions, she heard children squealing outside her tent door.

"Abimelech! Abimelech!" they screamed, and she looked out to see a camp guard leading him and two men toward Isaac's tent.

How long would the Philistine king trouble them? Goad them to other fields, if he planned such?

She wished someone could be with Isaac, to listen to whatever proposal Abimelech was about to put to him. For he could not see well enough to read men's faces, where the signs of scam showed the clearest.

But Shuman was with the servants digging and Jacob was with the herds and Esau had gone out to find Ishmael's tribe, living now somewhere between Beer-sheba and the mount of Seir, so Isaac had been told.

They had no more than settled in when Esau became his restless self, making his plans to go find his uncle.

She decided to scoot across the aisle to Isaac's tent herself, and stick her head to his wall. She could hear every word said in there.

To her surprise, she heard only cordial, amicable sounds among the masculine mutterings. At least all was friendly inside, and that was what she wanted to find out. She returned to her own tent, lest someone see her slipping an ear to the men's business.

But hardly was she inside her tent again when Isaac summoned her.

She girded a full robe at her waist and flattened it across her stomach, wondering at Isaac's unusual request—her presence in the midst of men. Since she had no time to groom and comb her hair, she twisted it into quick plaits that fell over her shoulders. And placing a fresh headcloth over her head, she hurried to Isaac's tent.

She felt ill at ease entering the men's company, but she pressed quietly inside his tent door anyway, and as quietly against his wall.

"They've come to make a peace treaty with us, my dear," Isaac greeted her entering. "They've seen what our God has done for us, and they say they will harm us no more if we will keep our servants from them."

"I've promised a new covenant," Abimelech said, then pointed out the men in turn. "This is Ahuzzath and this is Phichol."

She bowed modestly, but she would remember not to chat with them.

"Make a feast for King Abimelech and his men," Isaac commanded, slapping his knee in hearty benevolence, "and see they have tents for the night. Tomorrow they will depart our camp in peace."

"Yes, my lord," she curtsied, while her heart beat against her ribs. And outside, in the air again, she walked briskly, routing servants to start the meal that would celebrate their land of peace, for once Abimelech had eaten of their food he was not supposed to harm them.

She would see he ate of theirs in good measure. And next day, at the very hour Abimelech and his men had taken their leave, Jacob came running with some of the servants, bringing more good news: the great well was gushing clear water!

"That's my father's Sheba," Isaac grinned, opening and closing his spent eyes, "the sweetest water that ever flowed."

Suddenly he lifted his face to the sky, as if he could see its blueness without trouble, could embrace its billowy vapor with his outstretched arms. *How very much like Jacob*, Rebekah thought, that day in her memory when the earth was so dry and then miraculously saturated with rain, and Jacob had opened his arms to it.

The expression on the old face this day was so nearly like that on the young face that day it brought tears to her eyes, then to her cheeks, as again she saw their Ab, with his rapturous, uplifted gaze.

"Dearest Jacob," she murmured into her palms, burying her face into them, "somehow, you must have your birthright . . . together we must see to that."

Chapter 31

Peaceful days at Beer-sheba moved into peaceful months. A new spring brought plenteous grazing, while flowering shrubs and narcissus and poppies and splotches of daisies dotted the knolls and valleys around the camp. Leeks and onions and lentils and beans grew in abundance, and the harvests of orchards and crops filled Rebekah's heart with elation.

She held their good fortune to her bosom, turning much of her responsibility to the servant women, putting one to see that the spinning was done on time so the weaving could follow, and another in charge of the meal and flour.

No longer did she oversee the grinding. She had decided that the aroma of freshly ground grain was for the young at heart, when plans were made and dreams were worked at; and at last she had learned to trust the cleaning of the grain to the servant women.

Even so, she felt a need now of even more time, for life was claiming its payment for her emancipated youth—Deborah's health was failing; and Isaac, his sight completely gone, stayed mostly within the tents. He left his own planning for the camp to Shuman and the servants, believing each day was sufficient to meet its own calamities; a premise, he allowed, that came with old age.

But their quiet world beside the great Sheba had been interrupted, as Rebekah feared it would be, by the orgies on the hill just north of the camp, and since the day Isaac had turned the tribe from the Gerar valley, she had dreaded them.

She knew Esau romped with the wine in the village, and knew, too, that he had taken to the hill where ceremonies around graven animals and graven naked goddesses, with their firm breasts and rounding bellies, occurred regularly.

Isaac was disturbed by the tales that came to him about the place, tempting even the older sons of the servants to slip away there. But he had left the disciplining of his servants to their fathers, and had never thrashed them for anything.

"Reproof is better," he always said, "better than stripes any day."

That was her Isaac, Rebekah thought, the peace lover. Certainly idols held no powers over his life, nor her own, though they had been a part of it. The babbling of her father over his collection of images in the family teraphim had fallen on her ears often, but never on her heart.

Who could believe in the tiny dolls that could not speak? And if they could not speak to her, they surely could not hear her as her Yahweh did.

If her Esau could only know Yahweh as she and his father did, he would have no need of the hill.

"Oh, my Yahweh, that he might live before thee," she wept on her skins one morning early, soon after she had learned of his visits there, and then slapped her hands to her mouth.

That was Ab's prayer for Ishmael. She heard it from his very mouth at his tent door in early day, when she and Isaac had first lived in Sarah's tent.

How Ab had suffered in his family problems, sending Ishmael into the wilds, but still holding him in his heart, as he must have held the children of his second family.

But he sent them all away from Isaac, though with provisions.

So hard he had wrestled with his heart to keep the seed of Yahweh's promise pure and undefiled.

It was a struggle she herself was learning more of every day.

Chapter 32

Winter brought out her needle again. She had waited in anticipation for the tenting months, and now her felt walls wrapped her in silence. Isaac sometimes came to sit with her while she worked; but he could sense her concentration and would soon return to his more comfortable surroundings, or to his tent door, where he sat to listen, knowing the actions in his camp by its voices.

How she had waited to put her hands into the new purple linen the servants had woven for her in summers past, and this winter she vowed to get to it.

She held the fabric in front of her, fabric for her sons' wedding robes, planned already in her mind. She saw it draped about Jacob's heavy shoulders, which slumped slightly from hunkering too long beside his sheep; or over the fuzzy square shoulders of Esau, thrust backward in defiance.

Beneath Esau's scrubby face and fiery hair, the robe's purple shade was disturbing; but against Jacob's olive skin with his black shiny beard lying smooth upon it, its opulence glowed favorably back at her.

She'd had to send to the village dyer for the stain to tint the yarn, and paid a price far above her head for the royal shade from mollusks. But her sons would have proper wedding garments, and the choice of color for them was her own.

And they would have wedding feasts, although not so elaborate as the one Ab held for their father and her.

As soon as the last stitch on the robe for Esau was finished, she would insist that Isaac make arrangements about a wife for him. The time was upon them for that, and had been, but with their wanderings among the Philistines. . . .

She sighed and sewed on. And now, with Isaac's sight gone, so much more was going to be upon her. Possibly most of the arrangement would be her own doing. But his robe would be ready.

She decided she must rush her task on, or spring would catch her still stitching, and she called in the servants to do what they could to help.

Of course she would have Ruth help, or rather Ruth would have it so. Her quick hands moved like leopards so swiftly she pushed the needles in and out of the fine fabric, working too quietly for Rebekah.

On some days Rebekah felt foolish as they worked, and even more foolish trying to talk to her.

Never had she mentioned Esau's attention to Uma—or Uma's to him, Rebekah decided early—but she knew Ruth had worried much about the girl, and soon after her puberty Shuman had made arrangements for a husband, with Isaac's consent.

Now the girl was behaving herself quite well as a wife and mother—nature's trick to females, giving them the rein and then drawing it in too quickly.

"Do you think this shade of purple is too dark?" she asked, trying to begin a conversation.

Ruth shook her head. "The shade is eloquent."

"But you know me," Rebekah laughed, "I like my shades softened."

"It is fine, my lady." Rebekah glanced at her set face. The color purple for Esau . . . that was the problem. She felt a bit shy herself at the shade, but what she did for one son she must do for the other.

To make one robe of purple and one of another color did not seem right. She held the piece she was sewing in front of her a moment, then laid it over her knees again, smoothing it with her fingers.

Jacob would be ready for his one day, too. Her fingers picked up speed. And each son must have a strip of fabric enough for a turban, and a tiny piece of jewelry at the front, a clip . . . an ornament. . . .

Chapter 33

The strain on Isaac's face as the winter had moved on was becoming unbearable, and Rebekah feared he was turning ill. She determined to spend more time in his tent, to cheer him up. And on better days she took his hand and walked with him outside. She knew what was wrong, the spring was coming on. Changing seasons always saddened him, now that his sight had rendered him so dependent and inactive.

She had fought so against that, but the best he would manage now to do alone was to walk about the grounds with his cane, feeling his way with care. And when Prince was about—which was only when Jacob was—she worried that he might trip over the dog, for Prince would saunter close to him, edge against his knees, as if offering his comfort.

Sometimes then the dog would stand back, turn his head to the side, and study Isaac's face, as if he knew exactly what was wrong.

So she walked with Isaac when she could, and she spent nights in his tent, more so than she had usually done, for he needed her comfort in his darkness, that would never know another dawn.

"My lord, you know we must talk about Esau," she said to him one night, as they had lain down on his mat for the night.

"What has he done now?"

"It's what he has not done."

"You're planning a wife for him."

She smiled and scooted closer. "Well, you know we must. You told me yourself that he should have been with a wife already, and I have his wedding robe finished and I want him to have a feast and I have a wife in mind—"

"Ohooo," Isaac chuckled, twitching his mustache in a turn that she had always treasured when he teased her, and she raised her head to quickly kiss his cheek.

"It's my brother Laban's daughters, my lord. You know he has two."

Isaac's dry beard brushed her ear as he moved his head up and down, and she knew he was going to agree with her.

"We want Esau to make a good marriage within our family, don't we?"

"Except for the . . . the teraphim."

"But his wife will embrace our faith back here with us, the way I did yours and Ab's."

She felt a flush over her body at the statement, knowing it was not all true—but Isaac didn't.

The rising water, the Voice in her pregnancy, her elder son to serve her younger. None of these her Isaac had known about. And even now, she wasn't sure he should have.

"Our Yahweh led your father and me out of the ways of my people, and perhaps He will lead our sons' wives. Then Esau may—"

By now Isaac's arms had tightened about her. She felt the racing of his heart against her bosom, stirring her own emotions, and in the dimness of his oil lamp she forgot his troubled eyes.

It was a unity she could wish for both her sons, and their wives.

Chapter 34

Esau did not wait for her planning, however, in choosing a wife; he let it be known he had made his own selection, a Canaanite from ancestor Noah's Ham, and neither his father's words nor hers to him had changed his mind. But at least she and Isaac would take comfort in his settling down, for they had worried so about him, and felt helpless at his visits to the sensual rites on the hill, and his hunting sprees to Seir, where he stayed for days around shameless women and fell upon them at will, so the servant boys told of him.

She helped him ready a tent for his Judith, and spoke to him again about grieving his father at marrying a Hittite . . . a Canaanite.

"You know about the seeds of Shem, Esau. You are not to wed the seeds of Ham."

"Hah! That old story, Mama! I'm tired of hearing tales. All my life I've heard tales."

He scuffed his feet over the fresh grass where they were laying new rugs, and glared at her in impatience. She felt his eyes burning into her back while she laid a newly woven mat on the rugs.

She knew she was wasting her breath. "Well, at least I have your robe ready," she told him.

"And your father and I will of course provide a feast, invite your friends . . . and a number from the village."

He looked at her with a sly defiance even in that, but she made her preparations nonetheless, starting the servants early in their labors for the celebration, for she wanted all to go well on the feast day.

But after her plans had been laid and the mutton and beef and lentils and peas were stewing, and sweets and fruits had been laid out on the table Shuman and the servants had set up, Esau announced that there would be no "proper wedding," as she called it, for him, and he tossed his purple robe in a heap at her feet.

He would go for his Judith and bring her to their camp in his own manner, so he told her.

And he did, with his deerskin skirt about his loins.

Chapter 35

A few months later, Esau took a second wife, Bashemath. Rebekah thought he did so to prove his manhood, or, perhaps, still in defiance of parental authority, for Bashemath was a Canaanite, too. But she could cook, a talent Judith could scarcely claim.

Rebekah pondered that blessing at least while she helped him get the second tent ready. Two Canaanite women in tents side by side! About as much of an affront to Ab and his teachings on intermarriage as was Esau's hunting spree on the day his grandfather lay dying.

She hurt so when she thought about it, when she looked at Esau's wives, openly flaunting their smooth shoulders, while their kohled gray eyes watched him suggestively. And their balls of myrrh always dangled at their throats, where their warm bodies kept its scent trailing after them.

Esau would look greedily after them in the middle of the day, the yellow flame in his eyes kindled by their every step, as they tried to outdo one another with the roll of their hips in their tight-fitting tunics.

But soon the tight tunics turned to loose ones, for both Judith and Bashemath found themselves with young, and Rebekah found it hard to watch the rounding of their bellies, a rising that should have brought her joy.

How was she ever to love these seeds of Ham? But she was sure she would. So long she had waited to feel her grandchildren in her arms, to feel their soft fine hair turned under her chin as she rocked her shoulders back and forth, from side to side, the way Deborah had done the twins, with a touch to their bodies different from her own. That was what she wanted for her grandchildren, too, a special touch like Deborah's.

But now they would be an insult to Ab himself, and certainly to Isaac, after all his instruction to Esau.

She wiped her eyes at this terrible affront, and prayed that Yahweh would not punish the family for the sins of Esau.

Esau to head a nation. The thought was like lead inside her. With a nature such as his, what kind of humanity would he leave to earth?

One thing was sure in her mind—Ab's and Isaac's infinite faith must not be desecrated. It must be sustained, stimulated, and with Esau in charge of the family it would not be so.

The rituals of the faithful laid down to them by his grandfather were as futile for him as the dead coals after their celebrations were over, and she was certain he came away from the altar as unfulfilled as when he arrived there. And his wives never even bothered to attend Isaac's ceremonies.

No, she could never allow the precious promised seed from Yahweh to be scattered through Esau. Once planted, the seeds would sprout, and sprouted, like the precious seed grain Isaac hoarded yearly, would produce their own rebirth.

She would have to think, have to plan. But she feared she had waited too long now to talk to Isaac about placing the birthright blessing upon Jacob, for now her husband's face had begun to take on a strange blankness, as if he had blocked out all that was going on about him.

He left his low stool beside his tent door more often than he sat there now, and on some days his very mind seemed hollow. And aside from the pain of looking at his eyes, which no longer looked at her, that of his failing memory, too, was overwhelming her, overshadowing her days.

She seemed alone, the peaceful world they had shared gone from Isaac's mind, darkened as if by the same curtain that had shut back his sight. They couldn't talk on such days, and then the next day his memory would seem returned to him, and they would pick up the snatches of their lives.

There was a strangeness in her heart toward Isaac at his confusion, and she would have to adjust to it . . . and to him.

No longer could she go to his bed; she buried her face into her pillows and wept instead.

If she could only talk to him, tell him what was happening to them, and that she feared he might die without having passed on the birthright blessing. And if only she *could* persuade him to pass it to Jacob, keep it from Esau's wives; for if it went to Esau, it would be for his wives' sons, too.

She would need to watch and listen now, know every time Esau entered Isaac's tent, lest he, in one of his clear days, relinquish his cherished treasure to Esau's empty hands.

Chapter 36

"Y̲ou need to spend more time with your father," she told Jacob, when he was gulping down his morning meal before moving his herd of sheep to a fresh pasture. Summer and the herd together had turned the grasses in the highlands into stubble.

"He's lonely," she added, placing Jacob's scrip of food for his noon meal beside him, since he would be with the herds all day.

"And Esau has little time for him now."

"Does his mind seem any better?"

"On some days. Others, not so."

"It's Judith and Bashemath."

She drew in a long, weary breath. She worried so about him, about their life together now, of which she seemed too much to be in charge. She wanted things as they used to be.

"I don't know how your brother could have wed the seeds of Ham, after all his father's instruction."

"They sure do fight," Jacob grinned. "They're driving Father crazy. He can hear them, sitting over there in his tent all day."

"That's right. Your father's tent is closer to them than this one."

"But Father could hear them all the way across camp."

She supposed he could, and commented on his father's good hearing still.

"Makes his ears his eyes," Jacob said.

Yes, he did that . . . sitting all day beside his tent door, stool turned aside, keeping the sunlight from his eyes.

But lately he had left the stool. Jacob was right; his father *was* disturbed at Judith's and Bashemath's loud quarreling, which at times the whole camp could hear.

"Why is his mind worse one day and better the next?" Jacob asked, and she smiled a bit sadly at him.

So much she would say to him, this ruddy son with his firm flesh, whose body was strong from walking, whose leg muscles, with his every step, fairly ridged the thongs that held his sandals.

How could she tell him about the work of aging, which flashed the memory back and forth. That could too soon turn him into his father.

But standing before her with the glow of health about him, her Jacob would never hear her.

"It's part of growing old, son. Your father is certainly not out of his mind, and why some things stay and some go from it, I can't say. But they do, in old age."

"Oh, I didn't mean—"

"But," she raised her face from over the platter of food she was preparing for Isaac and looked sideways at Jacob. They needed to talk, see what they could do. "But his last days could be upon him, and—"

"I'll visit longer with him tonight, when I take his evening meal," he said, rising to go, and brushed her cheek with his lips as he left.

How she wanted to hold onto him, refuse to let him go, make him talk to her.

And she thought he was right; Esau's family problems were aggravating Isaac, blanking his mind even more on his bad days. And when she stepped across the ditch that separated their tents and kept the water from puddling around them in winter, she was even more convinced of it. She heard his agonizing groans even before she got to his tent door.

He had been awake all night, he told her. "Why, my lord?" He nodded in the direction of Esau's tents and said no more, as she placed the platter of food before him where he could break the bread and dip it into the honey himself.

She went quietly about his tent then, tidying it the best she could. But she couldn't move anything that he used daily; he became upset if he failed to find his belongings where he had placed them.

She poured his bowl of water for washing himself, placed his cloth for bathing beside it, and his clothing for the day, and realized he was not touching his food. So she sat down to assist him, reminding him that he must eat.

But he didn't have his usual appetite, and as soon as she had left his doorway, she heard his mumbles again.

The murmurs were the same sounds she heard when she had arrived at his tent, and she pressed her ear to his wall to see if she could make out his words.

Same mumbles, same words. "Blessing . . . blessing. . . ." She knew it! He was planning to pass the birthright blessing on to Esau, and he was in despair at his task.

But it was his to do, and he would do it; though perhaps from a keener vision, he could see their firstborn's future.

Chapter 37

"Father was still under his covers," Jacob said, returning to her tent after taking Isaac his morning meal. "He was still asleep."

"Your father's nights are troubled. He seldom sleeps now until after his morning prayers."

"Why?"

"He's not told me, but I think it's about the . . . the sacred blessing." She bit her lip nervously.

Jacob looked up from the mat as he seated himself, and she thought for a moment he was about to tell her of his and Esau's trade back at Lahai-roi. But he said nothing, beginning to devour his food at once, as he always did. He seldom went to the cooking tent for food, and the two of them usually ate alone, since Esau was no more with them and Isaac ate to himself.

They finished their meal in rare silence, and when he returned from collecting his father's bowl and cup, he said to her, "Father has sent a servant for Esau."

Their glances met, locked, refused to let the other's face go.

Quickly, she left her tent, going straight to Isaac's wall.

" . . . get to the fields . . . bring venison . . . blessing. . . ."

She wheeled toward her doorway. Her body shook, her blood left her, and she felt drained and frightened. She had to act swiftly.

"He's there," she said to Jacob as she entered her tent again. Her face had paled and her dark hair, with streaks of white in it, lay mussed under the yellow band circling it and her forehead.

"Jacob," she sucked in her breath, then let it out in exhaustion from so much thinking, "your father is sending Esau to the fields for venison. When he returns, he'll receive the blessing."

His eyes turned suddenly darker, and troubled, though she had no way of knowing what was in his mind, and he thought her eyes would never leave his face.

What would she say if she knew the birthright was really supposed to be his?

And was Esau going to tell their father now? Or would he ever tell him? If Esau didn't, how would he himself let their parents know?

Perhaps he had known all along he would be the one to do that, when the time came. And now the time was here. He knew it, but how would he handle it?

His mother was the one to tell first. Let her help him decide how to speak to his father.

"Mama, I have to tell—"

"Jacob, oh, Jacob, it's not right!" his mother paid no attention to his words. "You're the one for the blessing."

He couldn't believe what he had heard.

"Hear me, my son," she clung to his wrists with both hands. "Go to the flock. Fetch me two small goats."

"But why—"

"Get fat ones, the best you can find."

"We can only take the best kids for sacrifice. What are—"

"Jacob, we will make a stew for your father ahead of Esau," she spoke rapidly. "We must hurry. When he takes his father the venison, the blessing will be his."

"That lazy Bashemath won't know how to cook venison to please my father."

"Your brother hasn't forgotten. Now hurry! Dress the goats as fast as you can and bring me the skins."

"The skins. What do you—?"

"Jacob, obey me." Her eyes were stern upon him. He touched his throat, moving his hand along his smooth shoulders. She was going to make him hairy, like Esau! That's why she wanted two skins, one for each of his arms.

He grinned in relief. Now he wouldn't have to tell her about the filched birthright, nor tell his father.

His heart was a hammer inside him. "If my father feels my smooth skin anyway, I'll bring a curse upon myself and not a blessing."

"Let the curse be upon me, my son," she said, and her hands jerked on his shoulders while she guided him from her tent.

When he returned with the slaughtered goats, wrapped in an old piece of tent fabric, she checked the skins at once and set the meat to simmering, then gave her attention to the skins.

She spread the sticky, fatty hides with streaks of blood seeping through them over his naked arms and around his neck, where they lay warm against his skin, as if still wrapping the baby animals he had killed for them, and he shivered at their slimy clasp.

"I'll have to cut them in strips and piece them to fit you."

She twisted her mouth to the side as she measured, and appeared more at ease when she started stitching, moving her long needle in and out of his bristly sleeves.

"They must not slip," she said, tucking and pulling, "they must fit like the skin."

He imagined his father's bony fingers feeling for sight of them. Indeed they must not slip, and he stood with even greater patience for the measurements, while the silence about him and his mother—that could once so sweetly bind them—separated them in its heaviness. He looked away from her nimble hands moving on and on, and he wished they need not do so. "Go now," she whispered, as if another were in her tent to hear, "and return to me at noon."

When he had done so, the meat was tender and the covering finished to his mother's satisfaction, and she nodded to its snugness at his arms and wrists. "Allow your father to touch only the tops of your hands," she warned, tying the cord under his palms. "And he mustn't feel the ends of the skin at your fingers."

She turned her back to him then, grappling for something behind a curtain, and returned with an old mantle of Esau's.

"Here," she held it toward him, "the scent cannot belie the owner. Keep the hood over your head."

Jacob stared at her for a moment, sniffing the fresh pine nard on it, the same that Esau made to anoint his body.

"But what will Father think of a mantle when it's not the rainy se—"

"His mind is so disturbed today he'll hardly wonder. It's the only way—he mustn't feel your face and hair."

By now Jacob's hands were trembling so he could barely hold the bowl still, and apprehension filled him. "Wha—what if this doesn't taste like ven—"

"It has seasoning to your father's liking, and will be even better than venison."

She tucked a round of wheat bread into his hand and gave the hairy cover at his neck another pull as she stepped away from him.

"Make haste now," she said. "Your brother will have his stew ready soon."

Broth splashed over his fingers while he stepped to his father's tent, so greatly was he trembling, and he feared the servants would see him in his crazy garb. But he could not stop. He would not stop. He had always known the family should not go to Esau. Now was his chance that it did not.

In dismay, he stood for a moment at the doorway of his father's tent, wondering how he would ever get his voice to sound like Esau's. He made a noise in his throat, trying to set his tone lower, coarser.

"Father?"

"Who is it?"

"Esau, your firstborn. Come to bring your venison."

"How is it you've found it so quickly? I thought it would take longer."

"The Lord your God found it for me, put it right in my path," Jacob replied, in more than slight bewilderment at his overwhelming day. "Sit up straight."

"Let me feel you," his father said. Jacob tensed when the seeing right hand slid over his fuzzy chest, then moved down his arm to the back of his hand that held the bowl, tightening at his wrist. His grip yet amazed Jacob, as it always did, and he lifted the gnarled fingers gently, lest they reach his fingers.

"The voice is Jacob's," his father mumbled in confusion, sniffing the mantle in concentration, "but the hands are Esau's." He sucked in his breath over the meat and grinned.

"Got the sage and caraway right."

"As you like it, Father." Jacob knew he was remaining too quiet for Esau. His brother would have been boasting to high heaven at his catch, selling himself with his spirited laugh.

But it was better to be too quiet than too loud, Jacob knew with even greater certainty. All would be lost if he spoke too freely, and he kept that in mind as he stooped to put his father's hands to the bowl, moving his fingers awkwardly, so that the cord bindings crossing his palms did not brush the frail hands.

"Jacob always fits the bowl to my hands," his father whispered, as if to himself, while his forehead wrinkled upward.

"Art . . . art thou my very son Esau?"

"Of course, Father." Jacob choked back his guilt as he broke off a piece of bread. He dipped it into the bowl, soaking it well in the broth and raised it to the thin lips, expecting a frown, a show of doubt at goat meat passed off for venison. But his father's front teeth munched steadily up and down, while he chewed in his usual hearty manner.

His father sopped the bowl dry then, leaving greasy drippings along his long beard, and gestured for his wine. Jacob filled his clay cup from a full skin, facing with apprehension the moments to follow.

"Come near and kiss me, my son," his father said, thrusting his shoulders backward, and Jacob went to him, touching his lips to the hollow cheek, scarred with years and rank with the odor of the aged. There was something strangely holy about the smell, something that bespoke wisdom and pain and tears, and a queer sort of chastity, after so many years of living.

His father sniffed the cloak again, and Jacob bowed lower over him, moving his arms so the forest scent about it would be evident. He saw the thin nose lift, the nostrils flare.

"See, the smell of my son is as the smell of a field which the Lord hath blessed," his father said, and his trusting smile spread over his face while he pointed to the rug before him.

Blinking back tears, Jacob fell trembling there, under Esau's mantle that covered his head, which his father's fingers touched, lay upon, crawled slowly over. Quivering words poured over him, "Now, my son, may our God bless thee with the fatness of the earth, and plenty of corn and wine."

Jacob's face burned. What was he doing here? His heart was skipping beats and he couldn't breathe.

And he wondered how it was his father could have the sacred blessing so well in his mind when other things had left it; but his mother told him it was like that; perhaps the very important matters stayed.

"Let people serve thee and nations bow down to thee. Be lord over thy brethren and let thy mother's sons bow down to thee . . . cursed be every one that curseth thee, and blessed be he that blesseth thee."

Tears puddled on the goatskin arms, mingled with the fur, and when the sacred words ended Jacob wanted to go quickly from his father's tent, from the creeping fingers. But as he tried to get up they strengthened suddenly, pushing him backward, and for a moment, clung to his scalp.

"Guard the family well, my son, and may you . . . may you"— his father's voice faltered, and softened, Jacob was sure, in its hesitancy—"may you never bring shame upon it."

Choking back a sob, Jacob vowed he would indeed guard the family with honor, if he could do that after this encounter. Never would his sons and daughters forget their ancestry. He would see to that. He would teach them of their grandparents, of their great-grandfather Abraham, and of the woman who so miraculously bore his father Isaac in old age.

He would tell them of the promises, of the seeds pledged by Yahweh, where they themselves would number, and the covenant with their God they would know.

And as he rose to go, he brushed his father's cheek once more and turned away, touching himself in front with gentleness, and in the same awe that he always felt when he allowed himself to think of his mystically trimmed foreskin.

It was a thing he had wanted shielded from the minds of others, and only now was it becoming of significance to his own.

By his troth, his sons, too, would know its glory.

Chapter 38

Rebekah bit her nails and waited, peering from her doorway. What had she sent Jacob into? If her scheme should fail. . . .

She shuddered at the thought, not daring to take her eyes from Isaac's tent door. When she saw Jacob leaving, lifting his face to the sky and stretching his furry arms daringly, she breathed, "Thank you, Yahweh, thank you."

Her bosom fell in relief that Esau was not yet in sight of his father's tent. But soon he would be, with his bowl of venison sitting lightly in his palm.

She dared not think what might happen when he did arrive, for once the family blessing had been issued it could not be revoked. And there was his and Jacob's trade; Jacob might have to remind him of that.

A calmness came to her, a strange calmness, upon the thought of the blessing's security now in Jacob's name, in Jacob's life. And she knew it was. His elation told her that.

Her Isaac would get over this deception. It would pass, like other family problems, and she would be extra tender with him. He sensed he was such a problem to her nowadays, sitting idly in his tent all day, or hers, no longer asking her to lead him outside. That was what she could do—encourage him to go outside more. She would make a shade for his eyes, one that he could wear over them.

She had done what she must, for soon she would have to give him over—at times it seemed she'd already done that, and she could not have Esau and his quarreling wives head the tribe.

But she must get to Jacob's tent now, bring Esau's mantle back and dispose of the covering, though she knew Jacob would put it out of sight. And as she was about to go, she heard Esau's deep voice beyond Isaac's tent and stayed to watch him enter it.

When he had pulled the flap closed behind him, with the breath of his peppery venison trailing after him, she slipped to Isaac's wall. She'd not miss a word of their conversation, though the sacredness of Jacob's with him earlier had held her ear from his tent.

"Arise, Father, eat of my venison." Esau's voice was warm, expectant of his father's usual welcome.

But Isaac was clearly startled. "Who—who are you?"

"Why, I am your firstborn, Father. I'm Esau." There was a note of tolerance in his voice.

"You've been here. I felt your arms."

"Not mine," Esau chuckled, more amused than tolerant now.

"Who brought me venison? I've blessed him, and—"

"Jacob? You've blessed Jacob?" Isaac's voice would have shaken his tent then, had he been a young man. But now his words ran together in sudden, deep sobs, and she could almost see him tearing at his hair. "Yea, yea . . . your arms, but Jacob's hands. He fitted my cup—"

"Take it back, Father. The blessing's mine!"

"Nu, nu. I've blessed him and he shall be blessed. I cannot take it back."

"Then bless me, too, even me also, my father," Esau begged, like a whipped child. "No wonder his name is Jacob! First he grabs my birthright and now my blessing!"

She pressed her ear closer. Was he going to tell his father of the trade with Jacob? But he said nothing more of that, and Isaac apparently failed to notice his remark.

Her poor Esau. He, too, was of her flesh, and of her heart.

She had watched his little body grow into manhood, watched it muscle and harden. And how she had wept at the hardness inside him. This last blow would stiffen that even more, she feared. But would losing the birthright really be a loss for him? She prayed Yahweh would soften his heartache anyway, and would let her Isaac forgive.

In time, he would know this was right for them. He would see.

See? Her eyes filled with tears at her blunder. "Oh, my Yahweh!" she wept, pushing her face harder against the tent wall, "blinded by your hands and betrayed by mine."

"Is there nothing left for me, Father?" Esau cried, and she knew he had never meant to honor his bargain with Jacob in the first place.

"I have made him your lord, sustained him with grain and wine. What do I have left for you, my son?"

"Just *one* blessing?"

"Oh, your dwelling shall be the fatness of the earth, and of the dew of heaven—"

"We live well from the land already, Father."

"But you must serve your brother now, and hew your way with your sword."

Rebekah stepped backward. Just like Ishmael. Just as she'd always said. She ran sobbing to her tent, for she didn't want to hear more.

She wanted her bed, her covers. But she'd only been in her tent a few minutes when Esau went flying past it, his angry face set high. He'd find his brother, she knew, and their grueling fight would begin.

How shameful this problem would appear to the servants. She'd so wanted to keep Jacob's hairy disguise and her part in this . . . this sin from them.

She stepped outside to watch Esau storm into Jacob's tent, though in an instant he came scuffing out, mumbling and swearing loud enough for all the camp to hear, while Judith and Bashemath, their bellies cumbersome now with their young, rushed to his execrations as fast as they could.

But he paid slight heed to them, heading instead for the little knoll where Jacob sat, close again to the sheep.

Esau's wives panted after him, yelling over their shoulders at one another, Bashemath behind Judith in her walk and in her pregnancy, and Rebekah followed them, with her chest knotting in its nervous flutter.

She had to know what was happening to her sons, had to see, though their bloody faces were before her eyes already.

Trembling, she climbed the hill, and saw the first of Esau's blows to Jacob's head before she put her hands over her face, wanting to shut away the crushing fist, the drawn mouth.

She listened for Jacob's swift jabs, which at times sent Esau reeling. But she couldn't hear for Prince's yelping, his big paws scratching into the dirt as he danced up and down at their sides, and she raised her face to them.

Strangely enough, or perhaps not so strange, Jacob was not fighting back, canny enough this day to turn the other cheek.

"Next time, I swear I'll kill you!" Esau roared, licking his knuckles as he saw her approaching.

Then he turned and walked sullenly toward his wives. Prince followed him a few paces, but twisted back to Jacob, whining and licking the blood on Jacob's face while she cradled it on her lap, pressing her forefinger against the open flesh on his cheek.

"He'll be all right, Prince," she whispered.

"My brother is a poor loser," Jacob mumbled, trying hard to grin. And under his bruised skin, she could read his satisfaction.

Chapter 39

She lay upon her pallet and sobbed, burying her face in the folds of her arms. She'd blackened her name as a mother, betrayed her Isaac.

He'll bring a curse to me. . . . Jacob's fearful words rang in her ears. "Oh, Yahweh, help me," she wept. "Let the curse be upon me, not upon my fair Jacob. As to Eve, leave mine to me."

She would not get up, would not look on Isaac's trusting face. But it might no longer be so—he must have known she had helped Jacob. She heard it in his sobs, in his jerking voice, and yet he didn't attempt to revoke the blessing. And he wouldn't. At least she knew that.

How could she ever face the servants again, coming from their huddles with glistening, knowing eyes. Except for Ruth; Ruth's eyes had been warm and kind, when she'd seen her walking Jacob to his tent with his bleeding face.

A noise at the front caused Rebekah to get up and go to her doorway. Ruth was standing there, looking down at her hands in front of her, and her eyes held no accusation yet as she entered the tent.

"My lady, I . . . I have word that you should hear," Ruth said, folding her fingers first in one palm and then the other.

"I want to tell you that Esau is boasting he will kill Jacob." She kept her head down, watching her whitening knuckles where she had rubbed them.

Rebekah could have answered that she already had the word. Her heart had told her Jacob would have to flee Esau's wrath.

"He thinks his father will die soon." Ruth laughed lightly, knowing Isaac's hardiness. "And he says now he'll wait for that. But the way he's raving I wouldn't keep Jacob here. I'd send him off at once, my lady."

Yes, Rebekah knew she must do that, but not as a fugitive from Esau—she had to send him with the blessings of his father and his grandfather. And she must find a way for it.

After his father dies. . . . Well, Rebekah thought, when Ruth had left her tent, Esau could have a long wait. His father was not nearly so decrepit as Esau might believe, and she smiled slyly.

It was time to put away weeping. She had to plan, and her thoughts raced on to the terrible loneliness she would feel for Jacob. She had so little communication with Esau, and never would she have, if he found out she had helped in switching the blessing.

And certainly she had little in common with Esau's wives. If Jacob should take a wife such as Judith or Bashemath. . . .

She sprang upright on her mat. That was the answer! He could go to Laban . . . take a wife. She had planned that for him anyway, as she had for Esau, for she wanted one of her sons to marry a daughter from Laban. But Jacob's need for a wife had seemed so piddling.

Now it was time for that. And he would be out of his brother's reach. Ruth was right, Esau could cut his waiting short.

Tonight, she would go to Isaac, in spite of her trembling at what she had done. She would lie at his side, stir his sleeping blood with her nearness, though it had been so long now since she had done so. But first she would go to Jacob, tell him to make his plans for Haran.

"It will not be for long," she explained to Jacob, as she spread Deborah's poultices of winter figs over his face before nightfall, worrying that the bloody pockets under one eye and the cheek below it would worsen on the way, become irritated by dust and perspiration.

"When Esau's anger is turned from you, I'll send for you."

"Then the time will never be," he answered stiffly.

"Oh, yes, the time will come." She ached for him already. "But you need miles to your back now."

His deep gaze held her own, and she added, almost in a whisper, "It's too easy for the hunter's arrow to find the shepherd's back."

Still he watched her face, saying nothing, as if reading her mind and knowing she had more to tell him.

"And . . . your uncle has two daughters, you know. One of them should make a good wife for you."

"A wife? But I hadn't planned—"

"Then do so. You're a healthy man." She thought of Esau's wives with their kicking young inside them, living evidence of Esau's raging passion, while Jacob's seemed even yet untapped.

"But all the way to Padan-aram. That far land?"

"You'll be safe there from Esau, and it's time you took a wife. "I will talk to your father. Shuman says he's better in his mind today."

How could she tell Jacob that she had not dared go near his father all day, and that Ruth served his morning meal.

"Make your preparations. We'll get your clothing and bedding and food for your journey, and tomorrow you will be on your way."

Into the night, after she had given Isaac time to rest his body, she washed her own afresh, and opened a skin of her special anointing oil, with its redolent traces of spring.

Isaac loved the feel of it on her fingers when she caressed his body, and its fragrance about her skin when he caressed her, trying to love her in his darkness as if their youth had not flown.

She filled her palms with the soothing oil, spreading it over her arms and shoulders, along the front and back of her, and tucked a small measure of it under the folds of her robe as she pulled the garment about her.

The fabric clung to her bare skin while she eased, quaking, toward his tent, dreading to hear his voice, or have him hear hers.

She drew in a deep breath, as if it were her strength, and eased over the dip to his tent.

"... *it's not always easy to love a man, my Rebekah.* . . ."

Rebekah's eyes filled with tears, but she blinked them back, and whispered to herself, "But only in old age, my mother. . . ."

And she was not going to her lord for herself—she was going for Jacob.

She would beg Isaac's forgiveness, do what she could to make things right for Jacob. It shouldn't be so hard to do, for Isaac had heard Ab's dying charge to Jacob the same as she.

Ab meant for Jacob to follow on after him and Isaac, take the family forward, and Isaac understood that, too. That was part of his worries now, and she knew it.

"My lord," she whispered, dropping on her knees beside his mat.

His eyes were closed, resting themselves uselessly for a new day, while the low flame lighting his tent burned on, vainly for him, though not for others entering.

But the light was to burn on, unquenched, like his father's seeds and his.

A lump rose in her throat at her part in the great promise, though to have to sift and choose. . . .

"My lord," she called softly. Tears slipped from the corners of her eyes, hot against her cheeks, for she could no longer hold them back, and she whispered again, "My Isaac."

But he slept on, exhausted from his nights of unrest. She removed her robe, laid it with her oil of spring close beside her, and slid quietly under his blanket.

Sometime, before dawn, he would awaken.

Chapter 40

". . . send back him to me. . . ."

Rebekah stirred her wheat batter and thought of Isaac's words to her when she had left his pallet, quiet words, with a certain resolve to them, and a bit of pain mingling with determination. But he had spoken them solidly, without the slightest tremor in his voice, holding onto her hand when she had slipped from his pallet shortly after daybreak.

Now, while the sun rose over the east knoll, she stirred their unleavened morning bread, feeling her shoulders jarring as rhythmically as her wrists while the mixture clung to the bowl's edges and some of it splashed over the rim. She wondered what Isaac would think of her strokes this morning, if by them he could measure her feelings, as he said.

When her batter was well-beaten, she stepped from her tent into the morning air, and on toward her oven, hot and waiting for the bread. And before she poured it into thin cakes, she stood to look at the sun's rays across the yellow meadow grass, turning the damp blades into amber sparkles.

She drew in a quick breath of the morning freshness that seemed to offer her a pleasant day. But she knew better.

The first cakes were ready to remove from the oven when Jacob joined her from his own tent. She tried not to gasp at his swollen face, and stooped to remove the bread, then began to puncture and oil it and handed a platter of it to him.

"Your father's, " she said. "He wants to talk to you again."

Except for the bruised spots, Jacob's face went white. "He's going to take the blessing back!"

"No, you know he can't do that."

"Then what—"

"Don't be frightened," she told him, turning her head away from him a moment. "The way has been made for you."

She was so thankful Isaac had called Jacob to him again when his mind was unclouded, the way it was this morning when she had left, as if her companying with him alone had cleared it.

Now he would make it plain to Jacob that the blessing was indeed his own, and she was so happy about that. She could never have lived the rest of her life with the lie inside her.

And as Jacob moved ahead of her toward his father's tent, his shoulders barely drooped, she noticed.

She vowed she would not go to Isaac's wall, would not put her ear against it; she could surely trust him to do what he had promised.

But suppose he did forget his request for Jacob again to his tent? Or what if he became angry when he saw Jacob? Suppose. . . . She had to be sure.

Then she was stepping across the dip between the tents and leaning into his wall, straining for every word between them.

Isaac's voice was calm, as if Jacob's first visit ahead of Esau was no longer in his recollection, and in his old way he was talking to Jacob.

"You mustn't take a wife from the daughters of Canaan, as you know, my son. We want you to take a wife from your mother's people. She wants you to go to Haran, in Padan-aram."

"I know Father, she's told me."

"Her brother Laban has two daughters. She thinks one of them might please you."

"Would such please you, Father?" A slight silence followed, and Rebekah wondered what might be happening. But then

Isaac replied, "Yes, yes. It does please me. Go, our Jacob. And may God almighty bless thee, and make thee fruitful, and multiply thee, that thou mayest be a multitude of people."

The blessing of the womb! "And may He give to thee the blessing of Abraham, to thee and to thy seed with thee."

Rebekah gasped at his words. He had known all along, even without her insistence.

She returned in a flash to her oven and was setting the last of the wheat cakes aside for her and Jacob when she heard the excited note in his voice behind her.

"Father didn't take my blessing, Ma ma. And he added me another one, the blessing of my grandfather's seed and my grandfather's land and—"

"But it was to have been yours, don't you see?" Rebekah said, bending over the oven.

"You know about my trade with Es—" He hushed quickly, and she thought for a moment he was going to tell her about his bargain with Esau for the birthright. But he changed the subject at once, reaching for one of the larger rounded wheat cakes, which was only partly browned on one side and too much so on the other. No longer could she keep her mind on two things at one time.

"Do you remember what your grandfather was talking about when he lay dying and you sat beside him holding his hand?"

"Something about his heir."

"Yes, and he meant you. Your father knew it, too. Why Esau came first from my womb is a mystery. It should have been you. Your sacred mark told me first."

"And my father thinks I was to be first, too?"

"He is at peace with it. Perhaps now he can rest." She stirred the last of her batter again, slapping it against the side of her bowl, wanting to turn their talk back to Jacob's trip to Haran.

"Your father will give you ample gold and silver for your journey and for my brother's dowry."

"I don't understand about the dowry."

"You've got to show my brother that we have means back here to take care of a wife. But he will give most of it back, back to your bride, if you please him as a son-in-law."

"What if I don't please him?"

"Oh, my Jacob," she turned her wooden spoon handle loose and drew him to her, "you will, you will. But he will keep a portion of the shekels as a gift for himself and return the rest to your bride. But don't give it all to him. You must keep a portion to bring her back home on."

"Is my brother feeling any better about—"

"He is very bitter. Very hurt. And now that we are sending you to your uncle for a wife, he tells your father he will go to Ishmael, take your cousin Mahalath for a third wife."

"Hmmph," Jacob grunted, and grinned wryly.

"And afterward, he's threatening to take his wives and move to Seir."

"I guess Ishmael put him up to that."

"You won't have to worry long about Esau. With three wives to keep him busy, his rage will end soon enough."

She turned from him, so he could not see her face, for the pain she felt inside must be written there, and started toward her tent with their warm bread. She placed it on her mat, where they sat to eat together, and she would not dare let herself think it could be for the last time.

She couldn't bear to lose this son forever, as she had already lost Esau.

"And we can only hope that he will one day know this was right for the family. That our Yahweh will touch his heart, speak to him."

"You think Yahweh will do that? Speak to Esau?"

"Who knows? He could. But He will speak to you, Jacob."

"Me?"

"Yes, to you. I know we've talked to you *about* our Yahweh, and about our covenant as His people, but you don't really know Yahweh, my son."

Jacob looked fully on her face. Her creamy skin had turned more olive now, and a few wrinkles fit about her mouth and neck. Her dark hair, with streaks of white in it, lay smoothly backward from her brow, as if especially groomed for him this last day in her tent, and there was a fresh hint of fragrance that seemed always to go with his mother.

"But you will know Him," she added. "Yahweh will surely one day speak to you, as He has to m—" she stopped quickly, and her dark eyes held to his in a strange manner. "As he spoke to your fathers."

"Be listening, my son."

Chapter 41

"My lady, here's the grain you asked me to parch," Ruth said at Rebekah's tent door. "Whew!" the servant woman puffed, setting the bag down. "That ought to last him all the way to Haran."

"I doubt it," Rebekah murmured. "Haran's a long way from here and Jacob loves parched wheat." For a moment, the women's eyes met, then Rebekah turned hers away.

"I want to thank you, Ruth, for your kindness in helping me get his things ready on such short notice," Rebekah told her. But what she really wanted to thank Ruth for was her uncritical attitude, working on, not questioning this awkward turn in her master's family.

At times Ruth seemed unsure of her role, living as they did, bound so close to the tribe and so excluded from outsiders. Rebekah knew she herself had made the woman her friend, communicating with her as woman to woman when she needed to, and not always as mistress to servant.

Deborah came slowly from her quarters with her skins of mixed herbs and olive oil for Jacob's swollen face, and for stings and bites along the way. "You think two skins of ointment will be enough, my lady?" she asked.

"Put in three," Rebekah answered, "and three unscented ones for lighting his torch and for grooming. I don't want him showing up at my brother's camp looking like a hireling."

"He'll never do that. Don't worry," Deborah chuckled. Her fondness for Jacob had increased in her old days, yet Rebekah knew she still loved Esau. It showed in her tired eyes when she looked at him, and sometimes a sigh would escape her lips or a smile draw them to the side at Esau's boldness, at his open, rash profanity, which had taken second growth in his manhood.

And certainly Deborah waited in anticipation for the birth of his children. Rebekah's heart fluttered. She just hoped that by Judith's and Bashemath's time, Esau's anger would have lessened toward Jacob, toward them all.

Maybe the babies' births would help. And she did hope Esau's wives would allow Deborah to help with the babies, at least some, in spite of her age and trembling. But if he moved his family to the mount of Seir, as he was threatening to do, neither Deborah nor she would see the babies often.

What a dreadful change life was taking in their peaceful camp. And it would be so lonely without her sons, even without Esau's quarreling wives, now. Family was indeed one's greatest asset, be it as it was.

"Now," she said, wiping her hands on a cloth and getting her mind back on Jacob's journey, "I've put in his rounds of bread and his skins of wine and the oil, and packed the ointment separate from the anointing oil."

She placed the oil with his other belongings, to be balanced on his donkey as he would. "What else do we need to do? Oh, yes, wrap his bread."

"Let me roll it then," Ruth volunteered.

"And we've got to wrap his fruit."

"I'll go for that next," Ruth said, and when the bread was bound she started toward their store of dried foods hanging in the long drying tent.

"Bring plenty of dates and figs," Rebekah reminded her. "And some raisin cakes." Pressed raisin cakes were Jacob's favorite sweets, and she was about to forget them.

Deborah was underfoot again, trying to wrap the cheese.

Rebekah urged her aside. "Here, let me finish it." Her hands moved in swiftness, rolling the chunks of cheese in her worn linen cloths. Over and over and round and round she pulled the strips, sealing in the cheese's freshness, sealing in her heart.

And now she must mark Jacob's map. She picked up the top platter from a stack of them on her stone hearth, struck its fluted edge against the rocks, then found her flint stylus, for it would cut deeper into the potsherd. She wanted her directions to last.

She had gone over them with Jacob already, but the sketch was better; and she took a few moments to sit and scratch in his way as she remembered it from Haran, then laid the potsherd with his bedroll and clothing and waterskins and containers of food. So much to get together.

She pressed the clothing into tight folds, the nuptial turban, the wedding robe, inhaling the frankincense and myrrh she placed in its inner pocket when she had finished the garment. The fabric touched her face, and she breathed in its nobility. She could send it for her Jacob with good feeling.

Again, she saw Esau's crumpled robe before her, heaped and unused on her rugs. . . .

The scratches on the potsherd blurred in front of her as she moved it again, rearranged Jacob's clothing, his packs of food and skins of oil, and finally, the shekels his father had bidden her measure out for his trip and his dowry. Theirs would be gold and silver pieces, where Ab had sent jewelry and her robe and gifts to her father.

A daughter of her own flesh and blood. And when the children came, when Jacob's seeds of promise came to him. . . .

Her heart raced on, almost ahead of her imagination, for now the blessings of his father would be upon him: *Be fruitful and multiply*. . . .

Yet, one's fruitfulness was not always a certainty. And old age found one, sometimes, before a promise was fulfilled, as had happened with Ab and almost with Isaac and her.

But, the troubling part of hers was the pain it had caused her. Not the physical pain—one forgot the body's wrestling. It was the heart's struggle that left one faint; and wrestling one's conscience must be the ultimate fight.

And how was it she somehow put her own promise from Yahweh second to Isaac's? She had received hers first, and even yet, only she and Yahweh knew of it. But they were enough.

She was thinking too much again. Her heart had begun its quivering, like a butterfly trapped inside her chest, and the shakiness was spreading over her, intensifying as she realized all Jacob's bundles were ready, all his food was packed.

Chapter 42

"Perhaps you will need a third donkey," she told Jacob, watching him lay his bedroll and bundles across the donkeys' backs. She hadn't realized there would be so much to send.

"Father said take two. Here," he held out his hand for a bundle of oil, "that will fit right here."

And as he tied the bag of skins on to his growing mound of supplies, she stepped close to him, because she had to, and touched his puffy cheek briefly.

The wound was healing already. "Deborah mixed some of her ointment for your face. And you may need it for other bruises and bites before you get to Haran. Be sure to use it often."

"And don't forget to rub your arms and shoulders with the anointing oil, keep them from scaling—"

She wanted to bite her tongue at Jacob's glance. In the sun all day and she must tell him yet. . . .

"Rub your beard with it, keep it shiny." From the roll of her eyes, Jacob knew in her mind he was meeting her nieces already, and vowed not to shame her with his appearance when he reached Haran.

"Mama, I'll take care of myself."

"And watch the oil when you start your fires."

"I will, Mama."

"Dribble only a few drops over your handful of grass to catch your spark from the stones."

"Mama . . . ," he shook his head. "I'll be careful of the blaze. And of the oil."

"It's so important that you don't spill it or lose it on the way. Without your torch at your feet, you'll be nothing but prey for wild animals."

By now Jacob was laughing at her anxiety, as he had always done.

"And here's your potsherd. I want us to go over your route again. Just once more." She heard the weary intake of his breath as they bent to study her marks.

"Of course, you will go past Mamre and our field there."

"And I'm going to stop a while. Sit under my grandfather's oaks and visit the cave of Machpelah."

She knew he would do that, and she nodded, tapping her fingers on the piece of clay. "But watch now," she said.

"After you leave your grandfather's field, you will pass through Ephrath, and pass right on, don't stop in the city."

"Mama, do you think I would do anything else, on that rocky hill among strangers?"

To tell the truth, she didn't, as timid as Jacob was he would want to keep to himself as much as he could.

"But—do you think I might get lost if I go by Mount Moriah? I've always wanted to go to the mountain where my father almost lost his life."

"Jacob, you know better than to talk about that experience. It marked your father for the rest of his days."

That was true, if it caused Isaac's blindness as he believed, though they had never told their sons that.

"But you've told us that all of it was Yahweh's will."

"So it was. It was what Yahweh led your grandfather to do and he was about to do it, or thought he was. But at least he didn't have to. Men's faith—men *and* women's faith—is tested sometimes. But there are limits."

"My grandfather's limits must have outdone all others, then."

Or your father's, your dear father's, she wanted to add. "Anyway, he didn't have to fire his brush pile and your father is still alive. But no, please don't go to that mount. Wild animals will know no bounds there and you surely could lose your way."

She tried to hide from Jacob the shivers such thoughts sent to her body. He had not been far enough from home for such wandering.

She would never have to bother reminding Esau how to ward off wild animals. One could send Esau anywhere and expect him back—when he was ready to return—no matter how dangerous the territory.

"Stay with my route, and you'll find your way without trouble. And be sure to sleep with your sword beside you."

Jacob's restlessness told her she had talked too much. But she continued pulling her forefinger over the piece of clay, over the stars she had scratched for Jerusalem and for Shechem.

"Now you will have two rivers to cross, the Jordan and Euphrates, but the swelling is down in both. You can cross the Jordan on foot even, and the Euphrates by donkey at the ford. Just be certain you find the crossing. My marks will lead you right to it."

"And when you get to Haran," she hurried on, for she at last had Jacob's attention, "go first to the well. It's a strong well, like ours here at Beer-sheba. All the shepherds take their flocks to water there at noon."

How vividly she remembered. She wondered what had happened to Tu, whose wife she had become, and whose mother. . . .

"They will know my brother," she told Jacob. "Ask directions to his tents, right before the city proper."

She passed him then the bag of gold and silver pieces. "Now, slip this into your bedroll before you start. Keep only a few shekels on your person."

Jacob bounced the bag in his palm. "All this?"

"Well, a part of it is for your journey there and back, as I have told you. But keep it covered—at all times."

And while Jacob loosened his bundles to conceal the bag of gold and silver, Prince twisted about his feet, whining a lamenting howl, sensing that he was about to leave camp on an unusual trip, not merely one of a few hours.

The dog was still agile for his years, and Isaac said his mixed breeding had added to them; she herself had always declared him to have come from wild blood.

He leaped upon Jacob's chest with his front paws, and tried to lick his face, but Jacob remembered to turn it from him in its lacerated state. "You have to stay, my old Amir. You're too old to go with me. Besides, you're Esau's dog. He'll be mad."

He gestured for her to call Prince to her, but the dog paid her motions no heed.

In back of them, she could feel all the camp watching, except of course for her dear Isaac, who refused to leave his tent for Jacob's departure, though Jacob had bidden him a last goodbye.

Esau was nowhere about the camp that she knew of, but his wives must be peering from their tents; Judith's jealous green eyes would be staring at them even then, glowing like an angry jackal's, and Bashemath would be sizing up every gesture to report to him.

And since Esau was now married and soon to be a father, his absence from the camp no longer bothered Rebekah—except for today. Today it was a portentous threat, and she feared that somewhere out there even now he was bargaining for Jacob's life.

Jacob had rough country to pass through, inhabited by people with warlike eyes, and she had heard that killers among them could be bought for a song. Esau could be out there now, passing the tune's price to their waiting hands.

Oh, Yahweh, that my sons' beginning fight within me not end in the sword, she prayed. *And that they never father nations to carry it.*

Jacob was moving toward her, clearly with determination in his eyes that no tears leave them. And as he embraced her, she whispered, "My Jacob, how I have loved you."

"And I you, Mama."

"Be safe, my son. And may our Yahweh go with you." *Oh, my God, do so,* she prayed, *even when he gets past the people with warlike eyes. And may he ever be safe from Esau.* It was a prayer that would never leave her heart.

"And son," she added softly, "remember your mark. Keep it holy."

He swallowed slightly, kissing her and wiping her wet cheek with his hands, which were as gentle as his father's. Then he pulled Prince toward her by the leather strap about his neck.

She sat down to wrap her arms about the dog, holding him at her side, and Jacob took the donkeys' reins in his hands, leading them up the path toward Mamre, never looking back.

And when the laden dark backs passed over the grade, easing out of sight, Jacob's old Amir split from her grasp, topping the rise in a flash.

Her empty arms fell across her lap as she sat upon the summer stubble, tasting the salt of her tears and watching the cloud of dust from the donkeys' white feet and legs fade away.

Laban would be good to Jacob, and maybe he would even learn the warmth of his old grandmother's arms.

But in Haran he would be safe, and from his seed one day would come a great nation . . . a great nation. She knew that.

She had done what she could.